6

MALICE IN WONDERLAND (BOOK 6)

A Harley and Davidson Mystery

LILIANA HART
LOUIS SCOTT

7th Press

To our brothers and sisters standing along the thin blue line. We are a proud LEO family and love writing about heroic first responders. We salute you.

God Bless the Blue

**Check Out The COMPLETE List Of Books &
Learn More About Your AUTHORS**

The Harley and Davidson Mystery Series
The Farmer's Slaughter
A Tisket a Casket
I Saw Mommy Killing Santa Claus
Get Your Murder Running
Deceased and Desist
Malice in Wonderland
Tequila Mockingbird
Gone With the Sin

Chapter One

To Agatha Harley's way of thinking, there were two kinds of rich people in the world. There were those who were comfortable in their wealth, subtle in how they dressed and acted. And there were those who…weren't.

Buck Hazard fit into the latter category. His Dallas ranch was opulent and ostentatious, and Agatha asked herself again how she'd gotten dragged to Buck's annual Fourth of July shindig. She kept coming back to the same answer—*Heather.* Since Heather was one of Buck's ex-wives —his fourth ex-wife to be exact—Agatha figured there was nothing but trouble waiting for them, and she was wound tighter than a drum.

Heather didn't share Agatha's anxiety. She was eating little baby corn in precise rows like it was right off the cob. She kept telling herself there was nothing to feel awkward about. It was totally normal to invite all your ex-wives to the home you'd shared with each of them. Right?

"Stop," Agatha hissed as Heather started in on another baby corn. "Everyone is looking at you like you just fell off the turnip truck."

Heather snorted. "Darling, they're looking at me because I look every bit like the five million dollars I got in my divorce settlement and they're jealous. These people are all the same. Not a genuine soul in the lot of them."

Agatha looked across the hundreds of people who'd gathered over the green expanse of lawn and around the Olympic-sized swimming pool where the conversation flowed as freely as the margaritas.

"Then I'll ask again," Agatha said. "What in the heck are we doing here?"

"Don't be such a stick in the mud," Heather said. "Have fun. I've counted thirty-two eligible bachelors since we walked through the door, and they all have very nice portfolios. You should try one on for size." Heather waggled her eyebrows.

Agatha didn't figure it was worth asking how Heather knew about their portfolios. When it came to money and men, Heather was better than a crystal ball.

"I'm with Hank," Agatha said. "And these men would bore me to tears. Not an original thought between them. Not to mention the fact that I don't look like a Barbie doll."

The women who were working their charms on the thirty-two eligible bachelors, and some who weren't so eligible, looked like they could've been cut from the same sorority magazine. The dress was anything from star-spangled sequins to barely there bikinis, and Agatha looked down at her own little black dress and cowboy boots and felt even more out of place. She looked like wallpaper standing next to Heather in her electric blue halter dress.

"Honey, you don't marry them for their thoughts. You marry them for the diamonds." Heather shook her head sadly. "I just don't know where I went wrong with you.

You'd think I would've rubbed off on you at least a little over the last thirty-something years."

Agatha smiled, feeling herself relax for the first time. "And I love you anyway. Now let's get out of here and drive through Taco Cabana on the way home."

Heather's laugh sounded like a tinkle of bells. "We can't leave yet. Not until I know why Buck wanted me to be here so bad. He said he had something important to tell me."

"What do you think it is?"

"I think he wants me back. I might dangle him along for a little bit, but that ship has sailed, so I'll have to disappoint him."

"I'm sure his current wife will be relieved," Agatha said. "She's the one who's been shooting daggers at you ever since we came through the door."

"A little competition is good for the soul."

"That's a lot of competition," Agatha said. "Buck was married three times before you, and he's been married twice after. They're all here and probably thinking the same thing. I say we get out of here and let them fight over whatever pot Buck is stirring."

"It's not like I'm going to take him back," Heather said. "I just want to play a little and see what he's up to. You know Karl is trying to make an honest woman out of me."

"Does Karl know you're here?"

Heather pouted. "I said he's trying to make an honest woman out of me. Not that he's succeeded. Besides, Buck sounded sad on the phone. Like he needed a friend. And whatever we were, or how we ended up, we were always friends."

A splash and a scream over by the pool had Agatha jerking around to see what the commotion was all about, but one of the eligible bachelors had jumped in with a bikini-clad woman and she was giving him heck for messing up her hair.

"I'm just saying," Agatha said. "My gut is screaming over this. Stay out of whatever it is he's trying to drag you into."

There was no answer, and when Agatha turned back to where Heather had been standing, there was nothing but an empty margarita glass and half a baby corn on an empty tray.

Agatha sighed and pulled out her phone to send Hank a quick text.

Heather abandoned me. Wish you were here.

It wasn't long before Hank responded. *I miss you like crazy, but you couldn't drag me to that thing in a million years. Hurry back.*

Agatha smiled and went to find Heather. She had a feeling she was with Buck, and Buck should've been easy to find. The man was just past seventy, but he still looked good, probably with the help of a little cosmetic surgery. He looked like an older version of Troy Aikman, and even shared the same height.

Agatha wasn't exactly a shrinking violet. She was close to six-feet in her boots and it was easy to see her over the crowd. She didn't see Heather or Buck, and she let out another sigh just before all heck broke loose.

There was a shrill scream from inside the house that cut through the conversation and Eighties cover band like a knife. Everyone stopped and stared as a streak of electric blue came running out the back door of the house. Agatha shook her head and wondered which of Buck's ex-wives she'd gotten into a fight with. Drama followed Heather around like a dog in heat.

Heather's white blonde hair looked like it had tangled

4

with an egg beater, and she kept screaming as she cut through the crowd like Moses parting the Red Sea. It wasn't until Heather got closer that Agatha could see the genuine fear on her friend's pale face, and she was so distraught she didn't even realize she was heading straight for the pool.

Agatha started in her direction and heard Heather scream out, "He's dead!" just before she tripped into the water.

Chapter Two

THE WAIT STAFF FISHED HEATHER OUT OF THE POOL WITH the long handled skimming net, and they tossed a tablecloth over her man-made life preservers that had kept her floating at the surface.

There were snickers and looks of pity from the onlookers, and after the initial commotion, it seemed everyone thought Heather had just celebrated America's independence with one too many margaritas, so they went back to their conversations and the familiar sounds of "Come on Eileen" came from the band.

Agatha grabbed hold of Heather and moved her to the little gazebo at the edge of the lawn so they'd have some privacy.

"Have you lost your mind?" Agatha asked. "This is not the time or the place for drama."

Heather's pale face crumpled, and she started to sob uncontrollably. Some people might have felt a little empathy for Heather, but this wasn't Agatha's first rodeo when it came to Heather's histrionics. Heather could be sweet, and she was a good friend, but she was selfish and a bit of an attention hog. And if the attention wasn't directed at her, she was going to do something to make sure it was.

Agatha smacked her on the side of the cheek a couple of times to get Heather to stop crying long enough so she could understand what she was saying. "How many of those margaritas did you have to drink?"

"I'm not drunk," Heather said between snuffles. "He's dead. I saw him."

Agatha rolled her eyes. She hated to admit that they'd been through this before too. Heather had once thought one of her lovers had died after a rather rambunctious bout of lovemaking, but it turned out the guy was just sleeping deeply, and he didn't have his hearing aids in so he couldn't hear her call his name to try and wake him up. By the time the poor guy opened his eyes the ambulance, cops, fire department, half of the neighborhood, and the guy's wife knew he was in Heather's bed.

"Who's dead?" Agatha asked.

"Buck," Heather said, going into another round of sobs. "Ddd…dead."

"Are you sure?" Agatha asked hesitantly. "Honey, did you sleep with Buck?"

Heather gasped. "Agatha Harley, of course I didn't. It's not like last time. Buck told me he needed to tell me something. I told you that's why we're here. And why you were prattling on about your gut and feeling self-conscious about your outfit, Buck texted and asked me to meet him."

"Where did you meet him?" Agatha asked.

"In his bedroom."

Agatha arched a brow and sighed. "You're not helping yourself any. Candy is still shooting daggers at you, especially now that everyone's talking about you. Why in the world were you in his bedroom?"

"I told you," Heather said, the color starting to come

back into her cheeks. At least the expensive cosmetics she wore hadn't left her with raccoon eyes. She looked like a drowned cat who was about to start clawing. "That's where he wanted to meet me."

There was no point in mentioning the fact that meeting a married man in his bedroom probably wasn't the best idea. But it's not like Heather had ever listened to her advice.

"Come on," Agatha said, tugging on Heather's arm. "We need to go check."

"I'm not going back in there, Agatha Harley. You can't make me. I can't deal with dead people. I'm not a weirdo like you."

Agatha ignored the insult. Since writing about dead people paid her bills, she didn't take Heather's words to heart.

"What if he's not dead, or needs help?" Agatha said. "You can't just leave him in there. Plus, I don't know where I'm going."

Agatha finally got Heather to her feet, and they started making their way back to the house, ignoring the pointed stares and not so quiet whispers about Heather's sobriety.

The band was playing a mediocre rendition of a Tears for Fears medley, and Agatha felt a headache brewing at the base of her neck. They moved toward a private corridor that had been roped off for the party, and Agatha's gut started screaming a little louder.

"Always listen to your gut," she said under her breath.

"What's that?" Heather asked.

"Nothing."

"That's the door," Heather said, pointing to a dark-paneled door. "I can't believe he's dead in our bedroom."

"Honey, that hasn't been your bedroom for a long time,

8

and that's probably something you don't want the current Mrs. Hazard to overhear."

"Well, it's his private bedroom attached to his executive office. He liked to work a little, and then I'd sometimes interrupt him so we could play a little. Of course, at his age, he wasn't able to walk too far for either, so he had this private area added onto the house just off the pool."

Agatha eased the bedroom door open and she clamped a hand over her mouth and nose. The odor was so overwhelming her eyes started to water. It wasn't the scent of death that she'd expected. It was some kind of scent diffuser that made the room smell like a nursing home on steroids. A mix between Mentholatum and unpleasant bodily functions.

"Well?" Heather asked. She put a hand over her eyes and grabbed onto the back of Agatha's dress so she could be led inside the room. "I just can't look. Tell me what you see?"

"Did you touch anything in here?" Agatha asked.

"I'm not sure, why?"

"Because you're right. Buck is dead, and if your prints are anywhere they shouldn't be, you might be spending the night in jail."

Heather's knees buckled and Agatha grabbed hold of her before she hit the floor.

"Snap out of it, girl," Agatha said. "Time to be Texas tough. I suggest we call the cops." She dug in her handbag for a package of tissues and used it to wipe hers and Heather's prints from the door knob before closing it.

As they turned down the hall, a Hispanic woman in a plain black dress and a white apron came toward them. She was small and wizened and could have been anywhere from forty to a hundred. Her eyes were black as coal and her lipstick bright red.

"Shoo," she said, waving her hands at them like vermin. "Vámonos. No guests."

"We were looking for the bathroom," Agatha lied.

"Señora Candy says no one bother Señor Book," the housekeeper said.

"Señor Book?" Heather repeated, her Texas accent butchering the words. "I don't understand."

"Que Book?" The housekeeper asked, just as confused as Heather. "*Book, Book. Mr. Book.*"

"Ohhhhh," Heather said, understanding dawning in her eyes. "Mr. Buck."

"Sí, sí. Mr. Book. Leave alone. Señora Candy says needs sleep."

"Yeah, I bet she did," Agatha said, narrowing her eyes. She'd found it odd that Candy had joined in with the rest of the crowd in thinking Heather was a drunken party-goer, but if someone had told Agatha that her husband was dead, she'd have at least gone to check on him.

Agatha led Heather to the powder room off the foyer so she could clean up, and she pulled out her phone. "I think I'd better call Hank."

"And maybe I could have another margarita?" Heather asked. "I think I need something for my nerves."

"Try coffee," Agatha said. "It works wonders. Stay here and don't move."

Heather pouted. "I'm not a child."

Agatha just smiled thinly and moved off to find a quiet place so she could call Hank.

"Hey," Hank said. "I was just thinking about you. How's the party?"

"It depends on how you define party," Agatha said. "If it means lifestyles of the rich and famous invaded by the host's ex-wife, who surreptitiously ran head-long into the pool after finding said ex-husband dead in his bed, then I'd say it's a heck of a party."

There was a long stretch of silence on the other end of the line, and then Hank asked, "Did she kill him?"

It was hard to surprise a seasoned homicide detective.

"No," Agatha said. "At least, I don't think so."

"Wait, you're not kidding?" he asked.

"Because telling you someone died is my normal brand of humor?"

She could practically hear him rolling his eyes.

"Did you verify?" he asked.

"Yep," she said. "Dead as a doornail. I opened the bedroom door and saw him on the bed. I didn't see any blood or injury. But dead is dead. I closed the door and wiped my prints."

"Why was Heather in her ex-husband's bedroom?"

"She's innocent," Agatha said automatically.

"She might be a lot of things, Aggie, but innocent isn't one of them."

Hank was the only person on the planet who could get away with calling her Aggie. "What should I do now? Heather yelled out that Buck was dead right before she went into the pool, but everyone thought she was drunk so no one took her seriously. But they're going to remember she said that as soon as his body is discovered."

"I think you should call the cops," Hank said. "You probably should have done that before you called me. And be prepared to be asked a lot of questions. You're in the thick of it now, and there's nowhere to go."

"Lovely," Agatha said. "I knew it was a mistake coming here. What about Buck's wife? Should I tell her?"

"No," Hank said flatly. "Would you want that news from the ex-wife's best friend?"

"I guess not," Agatha said with a sigh. "I really wish you were here."

"Send the address, and I'll grab Coil. We'll be there before you know it."

The fist that had clamped around her insides loosened a little. It was nice loving someone who was always there for you.

"Thank you, baby," Agatha said softly and then hung up. She made her way back over to Heather, who was sitting in a chair outside the bathroom.

"Where'd that chair come from?" Agatha asked.

"Buck never changes anything about this place. There's a whole sitting room in the bathroom, so I stole a chair. Like people are going to want to congregate and watch whoever is taking a dump. Let's just say that that settee in there probably has more stains than a pay-by-the-hour motel."

"That's something I didn't need to know," Agatha said, squenching her nose.

"What did Hank say?" Heather asked while taking the drink in both hands. "Am I going to the pokey?"

"Did you kill him?"

"Of course not," Heather said, gasping. "I loved my little Buckleberry."

"Then you don't have anything to worry about. We're going to call the police and let them do their jobs. And we'll answer their questions. Remember you can always have an attorney with you. It's your right."

"But I didn't do anything wrong," Heather said, tears starting to well in her eyes again. "Buck said he needed to see me about something important. I just did what he asked, and now he's dead. What am I going to do?"

"I don't know, but Hank and Coil are on the way."

Agatha sucked in a deep breath when a dispatch operator picked up on the other end of the call.

"9-1-1, what's your emergency?" the voice asked.

"I'm calling to report a dead body."

Chapter Three

AGATHA WAITED PATIENTLY WITH HEATHER AS THEY watched the chaos unfold. Since Buck's address was high society, they didn't just send one squad car to check out the claim. They sent a fleet—all with lights and sirens. It was dark now, and the fireworks had started. Agatha had a feeling a whole other kind of fireworks were about to begin.

Agatha and Heather stayed in the shadows and watched Candy sprint toward the patio's gate to intercept the cops. She didn't look happy for them to be interrupting her party, but the two uniformed officers that approached her had obviously told her why they were there because all the color drained from Candy's face. And then Candy's gaze turned toward them, and if looks could have killed…

Candy said something to the officers and pointed to Heather, and they all turned and looked in their direction. Agatha had a sinking feeling in the pit of her stomach as two middle-aged men walked out of the bedroom where they'd been inspecting the scene.

They walked in tandem to Candy, and she gave them

the same earful she'd given the uniformed officers. They both wore plain clothes, their detective's badges visible on their belts and their weapons at their hips.

It didn't take long for their focus to land on Agatha and Heather. They looked hard. Agatha had spent enough time around cops to recognize the look. But she couldn't tell which was supposed to be the good cop. They both looked mean as the devil. She'd spent her career avoiding cops like these two, but it looked like she didn't have any choice in the matter.

"Heather Cartwright?" the lead detective asked.

He stood just under six feet tall. His black shoes were so polished Agatha could see her reflection. He wore navy slacks, his white button-down shirt was crumpled at the waistline, and his tie hung loosely around his thick neck. His complexion was ruddy, and he had heavy jowls and a shock of orange hair that refused to be combed down.

Agatha pointed to Heather. "She's Heather."

"I'm Detective Ritzo, and this is my partner, Detective Kraken. DPD Homicide Division."

"I'm Heather Cartwright," Heather said, southern manners taking hold automatically. She extended her hand, expecting the detective to take it, but he just stared at her coldly.

"We gathered that from your friend," Kraken said, raising a brow. "Why do you feel the need to have a mouthpiece speak for you?"

"I beg your pardon?" Agatha asked.

Detective Kraken was Ritzo's complete opposite in appearance. He was tall and lean. A vein bulged at his temple and she could see the rhythmic throbbing timed with his heart. His eyes were a muddy hazel and bloodshot. His royal blue polo was pulled snug across his broad chest, and he was preening for the crowd that had gathered around.

"I'm not her mouthpiece. I'm her friend. I assume my first amendment right still stands since, surely, you've only come over to ask us what happened, and you can clearly see my friend is traumatized by the event."

Ritzo snorted with derision. "Must be a lawyer. Or maybe you helped your friend kill someone and you'll both end up in jail."

Agatha instantly regretted her comment, but they were both so arrogant. No way was she going to be intimidated. She had done nothing wrong. This was America, for Pete's sake.

"Name," Kraken demanded.

"Agatha Harley," she said.

"Why did you kill him?" he countered.

"I didn't."

"What if I say you did?" Kraken asked.

There was pure evil in his eyes, and it took Agatha off guard. If he wasn't wearing a badge, she never would've thought he was a cop. Something was very off. She turned on her phone recorder before she spoke.

"Then I'd say you better read me my rights, and you and my attorney can have a very nice conversation down at the station. And then you can explain to your chief, when he gets my lawsuit, why you're harassing an innocent citizen who you could be asking pertinent questions to so you can solve a case. Unless you're not concerned with solving the case?"

Agatha's mind was racing as she tried to figure out why they stirred such a visceral reaction within her. She didn't intimidate easily, but these two detectives made her feel like her future was completely in their hands. Not a comforting thought.

Ritzo motioned for a uniformed officer to join them. The woman looked to be in her early twenties and still eager to do the job. Ritzo whispered in her ear, and her cordial expression shifted to a somber glare that teetered on the edge of angry.

"I've instructed the officer to take you into custody if you continue to impede our work," Ritzo said.

"You asked me my name and I gave it to you," she said. "What exactly are you going to arrest me for?"

Ritzo took a step toward her, but she stood a few inches taller than him. She lifted her phone to make sure her recorder was in a good position, and the female officer quickly stepped behind Agatha. This guy was a lunatic. He was actually going to have her arrested.

"Are you her lawyer?" Kraken asked.

"No." Agatha's lips were dry, but she didn't bother licking them to show her nerves.

"Then shut up."

Heather gasped. "Why are you being so rude to my friend? We know lots of cops, and none of them act like you two."

Kraken's scowl made Heather take a step back in fear. "Big deal."

"It is a big deal because they're good, honest cops," she continued, "Nothing like either of you. And they sure would never talk to us the way y'all are."

"Maybe you should date real cops instead of mall cops," Ritzo said. "Crybaby socialites think they can get away with murder because they're sleeping with a stripper with a fake badge.

"Are we suspects?" Agatha's concern tainted her words.

"I don't know, should you be?" Kraken replied.

Agatha wasn't concerned about Ritzo. He was Kraken's errand boy. It was Kraken that worried her. She'd known cops just like him. Deviant public servants who wouldn't blink at the idea of tossing someone in prison because he wanted to teach them a lesson about disrespecting him. She knew Hank and Coil were still about twenty minutes out, so she decided to cool it with the confrontation.

"Detective, do you need me to hang around?" The uniformed officer asked. "My Sarge is calling for me to stand perimeter."

"Tell your Sarge to hold on for a moment. I'm not sure what we're going to do with these two just yet," Kraken said.

"Now, which one of you was married to Mr. Hazard?" Kraken asked.

Heather raised her hand like a kid who knew the answer to the teacher's question. The hand shook nervously, and she hurriedly crossed her arms over her ample chest.

"Were you the last person to see him alive?" Kraken asked.

"No," Heather said, shaking her head. "He was dead when I was with him."

Agatha closed her eyes and let out a slow breath.

"Detective Ritzo," Kraken said. "Why don't you escort Miss Harley outside to get some fresh air. She looks like she's going to be sick. I'm going to have a little chat with the ex-wife."

"Agatha," Heather said, looking at her with panic in her eyes. "Are you in trouble?"

Ritzo reached out to grab her, but Agatha was quick enough to seem startled by his gesture and she pretended to trip. She grabbed Heather around the shoulders as if to steady herself.

"You okay, sugar?" Heather asked, patting her gently.

Agatha hugged her close and whispered in her ear. "I'm okay, but if you say another word, you're going to be in trouble I can't get you out of."

"What?" Heather said, gasping.

Agatha shook her friend and wanted to knock her upside the head. "For goodness sake, Heather. Just shut up."

"Let's go," Ritzo said, jerking Agatha away from Heather and toward the back patio.

All Agatha could see was the terrified look in her friend's eyes and Kraken started in on her.

Chapter Four

AGATHA DECIDED THE BEST COURSE OF ACTION WAS TO ignore Ritzo and keep a close watch for Hank and Coil coming up the drive. They needed to hurry. She'd never felt so powerless in her life. Kraken was giving Heather the third degree, but Heather kept shaking her head in denial, and her mouth was getting tighter and tighter.

The fireworks hadn't stopped just because of a dead body, and colorful explosions reigned in the night sky while cops and the medical examiner's team moved around the party-goers, who seemed torn between watching the fireworks and the live version of CSI. Since everyone was a potential witness, getting statements from attendees was going to take a while.

Agatha felt her panic start to rise as Kraken turned Heather around and cuffed her.

"Looks like your friend isn't so innocent after all," Ritzo said with a sneer. He turned his back on Agatha and headed to meet his partner.

"Oh, no," Agatha said, running toward them as they pulled Heather through the crowd and out to the waiting squad car. By the time she reached the driveway Kraken had slammed the door behind Heather, and the look he gave Agatha was smug and evil all at the same time.

The look Heather gave her was desperate and filled with fear, and Agatha was helpless to save her. She watched them speed down the long driveway just as Coil's over-sized, unmarked police truck drove around the barricade that had been set up.

She was running toward Hank before he even got the door open, and he barely caught her as she threw her arms around him.

"Was that Heather in the back of a squad car?" Hank asked.

"Yes," Agatha said on a sob. "This has been a night-mare. I don't even know what just happened, but if I ever get my hands on those no-good cops that carted her away…"

"Whoa," Hank said. "Slow down, sugar. Heather doesn't need a cellmate."

Agatha felt her muscles tense in frustration. Coil was talking to the uniformed officer Kraken had ordered to arrest her, and Agatha noticed she was a heck of a lot more friendly with Coil than she'd been with Beavis and Butthead. Though she didn't know many women who were impervious to Coil's charm.

Coil gave the woman his movie star smile, and Agatha almost rolled her eyes as he started walking toward them, but his smile disappeared into a thin line.

"Sorry we couldn't get here sooner," Coil said. "I wanted to check in and find out what's going on with Heather. I sure hope she can keep her mouth shut."

Agatha winced. That wasn't Heather's strong suit.

"What's up with the no-good cops?" Hank asked. "What happened?"

"Detectives Ritzo and Kraken," Agatha said. "Both of them are the most worthless excuse for cops I've ever seen."

Hank let out a long slow whistle. "No wonder you're so mad. It's been a long time since I've heard their names. I'm surprised they still have badges."

"They know the right people in the right places," Coil said. "They're dirty through and through and everybody knows it. But they're handy to keep around for certain high-profile power players."

"They only care about closing cases with an arrest," Hank said. "The actual conviction means nothing."

"I'm not going to lie," Agatha said. "I was scared down to my toes. It's like they hated Heather and me on sight. Do you think Heather's in danger?"

Coil hesitated before he answered, and it didn't make Agatha feel any better. "Only if she didn't kill her ex-husband."

Agatha looked back at Hank. "How do you know Ritzo and Kraken? You were all the way in Philadelphia and I'm assuming they've always been in this area."

Hank nodded. "I first ran into them while I was on the FBI task force, tracking that serial killer through Texas. It was around the same time when Coroner Sweet and I became friends. He was just a rookie cop back then, but those two crooked cops had their sights set on him as a suspect. If it hadn't been for me being Sweet's alibi, he'd probably still be in lockup, and for sure wouldn't be the Tarrant County coroner."

"You think they'll remember you?" Agatha asked.

Coil laughed. "I'm thinking they probably have Hank's picture taped to their dartboard. Ever heard of the Innocence Project?"

"Sure," Agatha said, frowning slightly.

"Hank made it his mission to work pro bono for them on any cases that Ritzo and Kraken were involved where there were prison convictions. Needless to say, Hank's involvement has paved the way for a lot of innocent people to get out of jail."

"Lovely," Agatha said. "So, what you're saying is Heather might never get out of jail."

The uniformed officer approached and had eyes only for Coil. She put a little extra *oomph* in her walk, and Agatha felt Hank choke on a laugh as he pulled her closer.

"Sheriff Coil," the woman said.

"What's up, Perez?"

"You're cleared to check out the crime scene. It's pretty crowded in there. Don't touch anything."

"I appreciate it," Coil said, tipping his cowboy hat. Perez beamed and went back to her post.

"How in the world?" Hank asked.

"She really hates working with cops like Ritzo and Kraken and asked if the Bell County sheriff's office would be hiring soon."

"Are you?" Agatha asked.

"We're always looking for good public servants," he said, winking. "Now if I could just get the budget to agree with my looking."

Agatha snorted.

"We don't have a lot of time," Hank said. He pulled his phone from his pants pocket, and Agatha noticed he still hadn't gotten his screen fixed. He'd cracked it after it had slipped out of the holder on his Harley Davidson a few weeks back.

"Switch phones with me so I can take photos," Hank said to Agatha.

"But what if Heather calls?" she asked.

"Then I'll tell her to hang up and call a lawyer," he said.

"Not helping," she said.

He leaned down to kiss her on the forehead. "I'll answer it if she calls. Don't worry."

"What do you want me to do?" Agatha asked.

Coil looked around the patio area and nodded toward a group of partygoers. "Why don't you get friendly with the guests. Maybe they know something."

"Try to play nice with the rich folks, Aggie," Hank said, giving her a wink.

She narrowed her eyes. "I feel like you're enjoying this just a little too much."

"I enjoy the thought of getting to take down Kraken and Ritzo once and for all. See you in a little while. Stay out of trouble."

HANK FUMBLED with the buttons on Agatha's newest model smartphone before activating the record feature. He documented as they walked through the ornate foyer and toward the hallway to Buck's private wing.

Buck Hazard may not have been loyal to his wives, but he sure was loyal to Texas. There were stars, flags, and Texas memorabilia everywhere in his private wing. That was one of the things Hank noticed after moving to Rusty Gun. He'd never seen a group of people prouder of their state. From bumper stickers to tattoos to Lone Star flags in their front yards, Texans loved Texas.

What he and Coil had to figure out was who hated Buck enough to kill him. There was no way it was Heather. She was selfish and entitled and flaky on occasion, but she didn't have an evil bone in her body. She couldn't kill a man in cold blood. Not to say that she couldn't do harm to someone if the circumstance was right. But not murder. She wasn't one of Hank's favorite people, but she was Agatha's friend, and he'd do what he could for her.

Coil lifted the crime scene tape in front of the door and Hank ducked beneath it. The bedroom matched the rest of the wing. This was clearly Buck's space. It looked like the Architectural Digest's version of The Old West.

Hank's eyes started watering the second he stepped in the room, and he tried valiantly to get a steady recording, but the sneezes took him by surprise.

"God bless you," Coil said, laughing.

"Thank you," Hank said, pulling a handkerchief from his pocket. "What is that horrible smell? My sinuses are going crazy."

"Smells like a hospital," Coil said.

Hank blew his nose and went back to recording. "I think that's the problem," Hank said. "You think Buck lived with that smell day in and day out? This is his own personal paradise. Bedroom, office, small kitchen and bar area, and easy access to the pool. He probably spends most of his time here. I think the antiseptic smell is just covering what lies beneath."

"You always did have a nose like a bloodhound," Coil said. "Too bad you have to suffer for the good sense of smell."

Hank stuffed the handkerchief back into his pants pocket and went back to recording.

"Let's get this over with before we end up having to deal with Ritzo and Kraken."

Hank agreed. He aimed the camera in one corner of the bedroom and slowly scanned the phone from left to right until he reached the opposite side of where he'd begun. The corpse remained on the bed, waiting for the medical examiner to transport it.

Hank finally zeroed in on Buck's body. He looked peaceful in death. Like he'd had too much to drink and decided to lay down for a little nap. He was dapper in white linen shorts, and a red, white and blue polo shirt. Hazard Texas, Co was embroidered on the sleeve. Hank noticed Buck's sandals were on the floor next to the bed. One shoe looked like it had been kicked under the bed. More than likely, the EMTs had done it when they'd come in to check the body, but it was something to remember.

From what he could observe without disturbing the body, there were no signs of struggle or trauma. There was something that niggled at the edges of his mind, but he couldn't grasp it at the moment.

What was it? Maybe it was the way his body was positioned. His body was in an S-shape, or a semi-fetal position. Laid on his right side, his head rested on his right hand, while his left arm was stretched behind him. Both legs were drawn up into his chest as if he were cold. It was a natural sleeping position, and one that wasn't disturbed as he'd lost his life.

Except for his left arm, and his shoe.

"What's bugging you, buddy?" Coil asked.

"Call me crazy, but it seems there's a whole lot of hoopla over Buck's death. You've got a seventy-something year old man, who I'm sure had been drinking, and he comes in to lay down for a bit and dies. Maybe he had a heart attack? There are no signs of struggle or an attack. So why are they jumping to murder?"

"I thought you paranoid murder cops always took deaths as a homicide and worked it backwards until proving that it wasn't murder," Coil said.

"We do, but Kraken and Ritzo would have seen the

exact same scene that you and I are looking at now. And they've already determined it's murder, and that Heather is their prime suspect? Something definitely seems off. It's just sloppy."

"So, you're not leaning toward murder?"

"I'm not leaning toward anything until we get a report from the medical examiner to confirm one way or the other. Taking statements and eye-witness testimony is all that can be done until then. Ritzo and Kraken should know that. But they've always done police work with another agenda in mind. We've just got to figure out what it is."

"We need to get out of here," Coil said. "I'd hate to see Officer Perez pay the price for being helpful."

Hank nodded as he went about taking pictures of the room, and then of the bed, finally zooming in on the body. He even photographed Buck's sandals. Just out of curiosity he peeked beneath the bed, but there was nothing to be found. Hank was thorough and liked to look at crime scenes as a system of concentric circles. He moved from the biggest ones on the outside and narrowed his search toward the inside. Too many people focused on the body and missed the clues that lay all around them.

Hank jammed his nose into the crook of his arm as he sneezed again.

"I think this is about as much as I can stand," Hank said, wheezing. "I got everything I need."

"Well, at least you'll smell nice for Agatha."

Chapter Five

AGATHA SAW HANK AND COIL COMING OUT FROM BUCK'S private wing and breathed a sigh of relief. She'd had her fill of talking to the rich and vapid.

She felt her heart roll over in her chest at the sight of Hank. He wore khakis and a navy polo with the FBI Academy logo over the breast, and she knew he'd purposefully worn it to give him a bit of clout when dealing with local law enforcement. She loved seeing him in his element. He might be retired, but it was obvious he'd loved what he'd done, and the air of authority came back to him with the ease of breathing.

Everyone on the patio was worth ten times more money than Hank would ever earn in a lifetime, but no one could match what he'd given to this country in the way of keeping sheltered people like them safe from the violent wolves waiting just outside of their gated communities. Hank was a hero, and he was her hero.

"Heard from Heather?" Agatha asked.

She reached for her cell phone, and Hank handed it to her so she could see there were no missed calls for herself.

She was anxious and worried about Heather. There was work to be done, and her best friend's freedom might just depend upon it.

"Find anything?" she asked

"Well," Coil said. "He's dead alright, but there's no sign of a foul play. The medical examiner is going to have to call this one."

"But what about Heather? How long can they keep her locked up?"

"They've got seventy-two hours to either charge her with something or let her go?" he said. "I called for the police chief, but the administrative officer said they'd pass the message along."

"What do you think that means?" Agatha asked.

"It means we've got seventy-two hours to clear Heather, or Ritzo and Kraken are going to trump up charges against an innocent woman," Hank said. "That's what they do best."

"That's three whole days," Agatha said. "She won't last three days in jail."

"It's what the law allows to give them time to put their facts together. Or not, but either way, that's a long time to hope Heather doesn't walk into their trap," Hank said. "I don't know if she can keep her mouth shut that long. She needs to lawyer up fast."

"Maybe you guys will have more luck with the crowd than I did," Agatha said. "The women have been licking their lips like you're the salt on one of their fancy margaritas.

"It's cause we have charm," Coil said, giving her a grin. "Hank and I are like chisels and you're like a sledge-hammer. It's because you don't get out much."

Agatha narrowed her eyes at him. "It's because the people in my books do what I tell them to do and don't talk back. Hank is enough of a people person for both of us."

"You and Hank are definitely made for each other," Coil said dryly, and then looked toward Officer Perez. "Hey, Perez. You mind if we ask these folks a few questions?"

"Might as well," she said. They're all speculating with each other anyway."

"Let's focus on the women," Hank said. "Whatever that scent was that was being pumped into the room isn't something a man would think of to use for cover."

"Good point," Coil said. "We'll split up. You and Agatha take the left side and I'll take the right."

Coil headed off toward a group of women that looked like they wanted to eat him for breakfast.

"Protect me," Hank said, pulling her close. "These kind of women are terrifying."

"I'll protect you, big guy," Agatha said.

He shot her one of his rare grins, and she leaned into him. And then they headed toward another group of women who didn't look nearly as excited to see her tagging along with Hank.

"Right into the lion's den," Agatha murmured.

"What?" Hank asked.

"Welcome to the ex-wives club."

Hank only looked slightly terrified as he stepped up to the tight-knit group. "Hi ladies, mind if I ask you a few questions?"

On closer inspection, each of the women looked so much like Heather it made Agatha gasp with surprise. Some a little older and some a little younger, but the similarities were unmistakable.

Agatha knew it was best to let Hank carry the ball in

this group. Exes could be vicious to each other and anyone outside their circle.

The oldest, and obviously more experienced of the group, looked Hank up and down, and a slow smile spread across her lips. "Well," she said, her voice sultry. "Hello, officer."

"Umm," Hank said with a deer in the headlights look on his face.

Agatha almost felt sorry for him.

"Yes, officer," another of the Heather's said. "Ask us anything. Anything at all. We'd love to help you."

"I appreciate your cooperation," Hank said, and then coughed to clear his throat. "We're gathering information about Buck Hazard's death."

"My poor Bucky," another of the women said. "I can't believe he's gone." Tears pooled in her baby blues and she fanned her eyes with her hand to keep the tears from falling. Her blonde hair was teased impossibly high, and her American flag bikini top impossibly small, though Agatha was grateful she'd at least tied a sheer red sarong around her waist.

"You were close to Buck?" Hank asked.

All three of the women giggled, and then remembered they were supposed to be sad. It was an odd dynamic because they behaved liked friends, yet there had to be too much history between them for them to actually be friends.

"Sure, honey," the oldest said. She was wearing red sequined shorts and a strapless top with long white fringe across the front. "We all know Buck in the biblical sense. We were all married to him. I'm number two."

"I'm five," the other one said. She wore a bright orange tube dress that barely covered the pertinent parts and a pair of eleven hundred dollar Jimmy Choo gladiator

31

sandals. Agatha only knew that because she'd had to look them up for her latest book.

"And I'm six," said the one in the tiny bikini.

"And it doesn't bother you to be here together?" Hank asked.

"Honey," number two said. "We're all set for the rest of our lives. We owe that man a parade. Nothing to get upset about. We all knew what we were getting into. Men like Buck are unique. He's a brilliant businessman, but a lousy husband and father. But he knows it and accepts it as part of a flawed personality. That's why our settlements are so generous. If Buck chooses you to marry, then consider yourself lucky."

"Some of us are luckier than others," number six said, pouting prettily.

Number two smirked. "What can I say? Pop out a couple of kids and the pot goes higher. It's not my fault Buck wised up and got fixed before he married you."

"Rotten luck," six said. "Everyone before me got at least one kid and a bonus out of the deal. Except Heather, and that's just cause she couldn't have kids, and he gave her extra because of that."

Her pout turned into annoyance, and a little line appeared on her forehead.

"It's old news Monica," number two said. "No use getting upset about it every time it comes up. Last I checked you were cozying up to some ball bearing billionaire. Maybe you can work a better settlement."

Monica pursed her lips and appealed to Hank. "Buck would add an extra million to the settlement per kid, plus take care of private schools, nannies, and all that stuff," she said, waving her manicured hand. "I'm just saying, fair is fair."

"Did you all see Buck tonight?" Hank asked, keeping them on course with his questions.

The women looked between each other, as if trying to decide who should speak for all of them, and Hank narrowed his eyes in suspicion.

"Let's start with you," he said to number two. "What's your name?"

"Oh, I'm Lorraine," she said, fluttering her eyelashes. "Pleased to meet you."

She was silent with an expectant look in her eyes and Hank prodded her again. "You saw Buck tonight? Spoke to him?"

"Oh, sure," she said, flushing slightly. "I spoke with him when I arrived. He said he was glad to see me. It's probably been fifteen years since the last time. He looked as good as ever, even for a man his age."

"What time did you speak with him?"

"Umm…" she said, tapping a long red nail against her cheek. "The car picked me up from the airport at 4:30, so I guess I got here around five."

"Where'd you fly in from?" he asked.

"Houston," she said. "The social scene is quite exciting. Buck bought me a ranch after the divorce. I always loved the horses, even when I no longer loved him, and he knew it."

"There were no hard feelings between you?" Hank asked.

Lorraine smiled beautifully, and Agatha could see the barely discernable crow's feet at her eyes. She'd had good work done, and Agatha wondered exactly how old she was since she was Buck's number two. She was probably in her fifties.

"Honey, of course there were hard feelings," she said.

"We'd have the best fights. And then we'd make love. Fight and make love. And then he decided to make love to Janet, who was wife number three. She was eighteen and very nubile. Buck always liked them young. So that was the end of our marriage. But that was a long time ago. My life has been good because of Buck. Divorcing him was the best thing I ever did."

"As I understand," Hank said. "Buck held this Fourth of July bash every year. Did you get an invite every year, or was this a special occasion?"

"This was the first invite for me," Monica said. "Of course. We've only been divorced for a year, so it was nice to have a little space from Candy." She rolled her eyes at the other woman's name.

"Candy?" Hank asked.

"Number seven," Monica said. "She's the current Mrs. Hazard. And I guess the final."

It was clear from the looks on the former Mrs. Hazards' faces that Candy would never be issued an invitation to their little group. It was also clear that wife number six had not come to peace with the divorce like wife number two had. But Monica was still very young. She was probably only mid-twenties.

Monica looked like she should be enjoying sorority parties instead of being a member of the ex-wives club. She didn't have the polish of the older women, and where the others were calm and cool and composed, Monica kept fiddling with the cross that hung around her neck.

"Did Buck give you that cross?" Hank asked Monica.

She looked down at it as if she couldn't figure out how it had ended up in her hand. "He gave it to me on our wedding day," she said. "Buck was a very religious man. Except for his inability to remain faithful to his wives."

She hadn't noticed before Hank had pointed it out, but on closer inspection, all the women were wearing an identical cross. He turned to the one in the red tube dress. Number five.

"I'm sorry," Hank said. "I didn't catch your name."

"Theresa," number five said. Her orange dress was out of place among all the red, white, and blue, but she didn't seem to care. She seemed quieter than the other two, her eyes more thoughtful, more intelligent.

"You wear the same cross," Hank said. "Buck gave it to you as well?"

"Just one of the many perks of being Mrs. Hazard," she said. "As you can see, we've all got them. When Buck called and said he wanted me to come, that he had something he wanted to say to me, I put it back on for sentimental reasons. I put on this dress," she said, outlining her voluptuous figure with her hands. "Orange is his favorite color. I thought he might want to get back together. I wouldn't have, of course." She was fast to reassure the others. "The past is the past."

"Do you think that's what Buck wanted?" Hank asked. "To reconcile?"

It was Lorraine who answered this time, and her honeyed Texas drawl was replaced with a hard edge of anger.

"Who knows what the heck Buck wanted. He invited us all here for a reason, without telling us the others were coming. Buck could be a charming son of a gun, and he was impossible to say no to. But I can speak for all of us when I say I'm tired of getting screwed over by Buck Hazard."

Chapter Six

HANK NOTICED COIL MOTIONING FOR THEM, SO HE thanked the ladies for their time, and he and Agatha went to meet him by the pool.

"Wow," Agatha said as they put distance between them. "There's a hotbed of undercurrents in that little group. What do you make out of it?"

"That hell hath no fury like a woman scorned," Hank said.

"He cheated on all of them with a younger model of themselves," Agatha said. "I'm sure that caused some issues. Even Heather has struggled with insecurity and her looks since Buck left her for Theresa. If you ask me, it's creepy how much they all look the same."

"It definitely makes one wonder about Buck," Hank agreed.

"You said Heather was invited because he wanted to tell her something, so that fits with the other's stories. He texts her for a meet, but by the time she went to see him, he was dead. It makes you wonder who else he texted before her. Was he going in order? And what was so important that he had to have all his ex-wives back under his roof for the first time ever?

"Money?" Agatha asked.

"Or maybe power?" Hank added. "Maybe Buck was the kind of man who liked to jerk the strings and watch people dance."

Coil was standing alone by the pool, checking his phone when they walked up. "How'd you make out?" Hank asked him.

"Not too great," Coil said. "I talked to a few of Buck's hunting buddies. They all said he was in the best shape of his life and the new wife was keeping him young. Of course, they said Buck had said that about each of his wives. The hunting buddies outlasted all of his marriages."

"Maybe he should have married them," Agatha said dryly.

"What about enemies?" Hank asked.

"They said they couldn't think of any," Coil said. "Everyone loved old Buck. He was a brilliant businessman, and always kept his word. At least when he was wheeling and dealing. His reputation is impeccable in the business world. And the indiscretions in his personal life could usually be taken care of with cash."

"What type of indiscretions?" Agatha asked.

"The man was a notorious womanizer," Coil said. "Liked having a lot of his business meetings at strip clubs, and he treated company getaways like extended bachelor parties. I'm under the impression women don't generally care to work for Buck unless they're looking for a romantic entanglement."

"He just sounds better by the minute," Agatha said.

Coil flashed a quick grin, but his eyes never stopped scanning the crowd. Agatha knew he'd worked undercover too long to ever feel too comfortable among a crowd.

"Well, we know Buck had money and power," Hank said. "Those are two pretty powerful motives for murder."

"*If* he was murdered," Agatha piped in.

"His buddies did say that Buck liked to gamble a bit, but after the SMU debacle, he's stayed out of sports and stuck to the high stakes tables. They said it was nothing for Buck to call them up and take everyone to Vegas in his plane for a few days. He owns a hotel on the strip, so it was nothing."

"SMU debacle?" Hank asked.

"The SMU football team. Don't you recall when they were under NCAA investigation for all types of violations. They got the death penalty in 1987, and the college had to terminate their winning football program."

"Oh yeah," Hank said, nodding. "I remember now. How was Buck involved?"

"He was deep in the middle of paying players and buying gifts for their folks," Coil said. "Then, as everything started to come to light, Buck tried to pay off the NCAA officials. It backfired and he was a social outcast for about a decade, but it blew over eventually." Coil lifted his Stetson and smoothed back his hair before replacing it. "Did y'all find out anything?"

"Let's just say his ex-wives have an eerie resemblance to each other," Hank said. "And I don't think everything is as smooth and friendly as they're letting on." He nodded toward the group of women and noticed two more had joined them. Must've been number one and three.

"I don't care what they say," Coil said. "That many ex-wives together can never be a good thing."

"There are secrets there," Hank said.

"I'd like to talk to the oldest one again," Agatha said. "Just us girls. She's sharper than the others. But I think she was lying behind that smile. I think she still has a whole lot of resentment toward Buck."

"Good luck with that," Hank said.

Agatha smiled. Hank loved it when she smiled. He also loved it when they were back in Rusty Gun and in their own space. He was retired for a reason. This crowd, though he certainly knew Agatha made enough money from writing to fit in with them, didn't suit either of their lifestyles. She was an introvert by nature, and he'd learned there was something to slowing down and smelling the roses every once in a while.

"I'm going to go hang out in the ladies' room," she said. "You know how they love to gossip in there. I'll text you if I hear anything. Plus, I can kill two birds with one stone. I drank a lot of iced tea tonight."

Hank and Coil chuckled as she headed back into the house in a hurry. They tried talking to a few other folks, but they did have any luck. The buzz was starting to wear off, and people were getting restless, so they ignored any attempt Hank and Coil made at asking questions.

"Maybe she'll have more luck from the bathroom," Hank said, exasperated. He felt a tug on his sleeve and looked down to see Lorraine standing there, smiling expectantly. He'd already decided they'd made her an unofficial spokeswoman for the group, and he wondered what they'd managed to cook up since he last left them.

"Can I talk to you in private?" Lorraine asked, eyeing Coil suspiciously.

"I'll be over here," Coil said, sighing.

Hank's brows raised as she hooked her arm through his, and he led her near the gazebo where there weren't as many people milling about. Her hands moved from his elbow and latched onto his bicep, where she gave it a couple of squeezes and purred appreciatively.

Hank swallowed hard and looked toward the house to see if he could find Agatha, but he was alone with Lorraine Hazard, and she was looking at him like prey.

"Is this a good spot to talk?" he asked, and quickly released himself from her clutches.

"Yes, thank you," Lorraine said, nonplussed by the distance he put between them. She took a seat on a rustic bench with a Texas star branded into the back of it. She let out a deep breath and look across the gaudily lit rolling land.

"I've always hated this place," she said. "Buck and his first wife, Noreen, built it from the ground up after he started making money hand over fist. They were married twenty years you know."

"No, I didn't," Hank said.

"Then I came along." Her smile was unashamed and reminiscent. "I had a job at one of those delivery service places. I'd wear a cute little pink and white striped skirt and a prim white button-down shirt, and I'd deliver everything from balloons to cases of liquor to the who's who of Dallas. I'd just turned eighteen years old and Buck was a little past forty. Lord, that man was handsome. I'd have walked across hot coals to get to him. He was powerful...magnetic.

"So, he and Noreen split, and we got married the weekend after the ink was dry on his divorce papers. I was so young and naïve. I had my whole life ahead of me, and it was exactly the life I imagined for myself. Going to spas and traveling all over the world. I gave him two sons, just like Noreen had. We lasted eight years before Connie came along. She'd just turned eighteen too."

Lorraine laughed ironically to herself, but the smile didn't reach her eyes. I thought we were building some-thing special here. We had the pool put in, and I put my touches around the house. I went to parties and learned how to be a good hostess. Any imperfections in my face or body were fixed by surgery, so I could be perfect for Buck. And he threw me away anyway."

Hank felt sorry for her, and he dropped down onto the bench beside her.

"It still hurts," he said with empathy.

She snorted daintily. "Every day. You'll hear it over and over again. Everybody loved Buck. He was a man's man, and he'd do anything for anyone in need. Except for his wife and kids. I don't hate him, but I do hate what he did. What he did to all of us. Buck loved us for a time, and then he swapped us out like cheap stocks with a promise of quick gain. Money can't buy everything," she said. "And if he hadn't died tonight, you can bet your bottom dollar Candy would've been out the door before too long."

"This is the first time y'all have all been together at an event like this?" Hank asked.

"Yes," she said. "But we all know each other, and we've gotten together out of necessity if children were involved. Noreen and I eventually became good friends, and I'm friendly with a couple of the others. We'll meet for lunch from time to time, or if we happen to cross each other's paths while traveling, we might have dinner."

"What made this time different?" Hank asked.

Her breath hitched, and she was staring off, looking toward the blue lights flashing in the driveway and mesmerized by them. "I didn't realize the others would be here. When he called me, I don't know what I thought at first. He told me he needed to talk to me. That he had something very important to say. I wondered if maybe he was sick or dying. But the way he talked to me was so sweet. He reminded me of the time we'd gone horseback riding on the beach, and he tried to lean over and kiss me just as his horse took off at a break neck pace." She laughed at the memory, and this time it reached her eyes. "He fell right on his behind in the sand. Buck was an expert rider, which is what made it so funny.

"I thought," she said, pausing. "Just the way he talked he made me think he wanted me back. For things to be like the old times. Then come to find out that's what the other's all thought too. He was screwing us all the way up to the end."

"What was it he wanted to tell you?" Hank asked.

Her back stiffened and he could feel the rage coming off her in waves. "It wasn't to get back together, that's for sure."

Hank sighed and patted her on the shoulder, completely uncomfortable with public displays of affection.

Her smile trembled as she looked at him with unshed tears in her eyes. "I appreciate your compassion, Detective."

"I know the pain of loss," he said simply. "What did he tell you?"

"That he'd finally found the love of his life. He was madly in love with Candy, and it was going to change things between all of us."

"Why would someone kill Buck because he loved his wife?" Hank asked

Lorraine gasped. "He was murdered?"

"Well," Hank admitted. "The detectives handling the case sure seem to think so."

She leaned back and looked him up and down again. "I thought you were investigating Buck's death."

Hank couldn't deceive her. He would be guilty of interfering in an official police investigation. The truth was, Hank had zero authority to be there asking questions. Sure, he was one question away from getting all he needed to know, but he wouldn't ever consider breaking the law or interfering in it.

"No, ma'am," he said. "I'm a retired homicide detective who was called in to help a friend of my..." he thought about it a few seconds, completely unsure what he was supposed to call Agatha. "My girlfriend," he finally said. But that didn't sit well at all. Agatha definitely wasn't a girl.

Lorraine's brows raised almost to her hairline. "You're here to help that devil, Heather Cartwright?" she asked sharply.

"I take it you and Heather don't make regular lunch dates," Hank said.

"If someone murdered Buck there's no doubt in my mind it was her." Lorraine straightened her spine and got up, her hips twitching to a rhythm only she could hear as she made her way back to the other exes.

"Well," Hank said. "That blows that shot."

Chapter Seven

Sunday

July in Rusty Gun, Texas was no longer just a warm peck on the cheek like it had been the month before. It was hot. Really hot. And though Hank occasionally saw kids out on their bikes or joggers out in the early morning hours, no one stayed outside for long. Texas summers were everything he'd ever heard about and more.

It was his second summer in Rusty Gun, and despite the spike in heat, he decided to hit the open road on his motorcycle before his meeting with Agatha and Coil to discuss Heather's situation. There was no word on what killed Buck Hazard, but Heather was still in custody while Ritzo and Kraken worked on finding something to charge her with.

Hank drove slowly through Main Street on his black and silver Harley. The heat from the pavement was so hot it could have melted his boots, and it curled around his legs, so it felt like he was being cooked inside his jeans. He wore a white undershirt and a sleeveless flannel shirt over it that flapped open in the hot breeze.

Since getting a clean bill of health on his dislocated right shoulder after rescuing Agatha from the line of fire from a sniper's rifle, Hank had become very comfortable handling the giant machine. Exploring Texas hill country had become his passion.

It was almost eleven thirty as he idled the HOG past what was once Bucky's Brisket Basket. The former icon along Main Street's strip had been closed permanently since its owner, Sheila Johnson, had been murdered the past April. Hank felt a knot in his gut. Sheila had been a close friend, and she was one of the few folks he'd felt comfortable enough to open up to.

Sheriff Coil caught his eye as he hurried across the street ahead of Hank. His old friend hustled into the café with a crowd of church folks. Hank wondered if Reggie had found anything else about Buck's cause of death since they'd left the party late last night.

Hank eased his bike in between two parked cars. That was one of the great things about riding a motorcycle. He always got the best parking spots. He thought of Sully, the pirate outlaw biker, and how he'd taught Hank a few tricks of the trade for making sure he got the front spots on his bike while also making sure careless motorists didn't ding his chrome pride and joy.

He'd last spoken to Sully a week ago. Seemed the old biker had recovered from his beat down by the Lone Star Rattlers outlaw motorcycle club. With a good word from Coil to the manager at Reverend Graham's Harley Davidson shop, Sully was back to work in the maintenance department. Hank's friendship with the ex-outlaw was one he'd never have imagined, but neither was living in a tiny Texas town in the middle of nowhere.

The bell chimed when he stepped through the door of the cafe, and he waited for his vision to adjust to the soft interior lights of a crowded café. He looked toward their usual booth in the far corner of the restaurant with an anticipation of seeing Agatha waiting for him, but there were unfamiliar faces in their usual space. He scowled. He was most comfortable with structure.

"Hank," Agatha called out.

He turned toward her voice, and there she was. He immediately felt more at ease. Despite having lived in Rusty Gun for almost two years, he was still a stranger to most people, and most people were strangers to him.

Hank hugged her, and he loved the way she fit so easily into his arms. "Long time no see," he said to Coil, who was already sitting at the table.

"Thanks for not running me down out there," Coil said with a chuckle. "You're becoming a regular rebel without a cause on that thing."

Hank finagled the chair so he faced the front door and adjusted his concealed weapon beneath his shirt. He adjusted the chair a couple of more times until he was as comfortable as he was going to be without having a full view to the outside.

If he was honest, he was a little paranoid about the Lone Star Rattlers motorcycle club. They weren't happy about him shooting some of their members, and Hank suspected there might be a bounty on his head. But he kept that to himself as to not alarm Agatha. She had enough to worry about with Heather in jail.

"It's good to see you survived the ladies' room last night," Hank said, nudging Agatha.

"Yeah, thanks for waiting," she said dryly. "I come out and all heck had broken loose."

"Sorry about that," Hank said, wincing. "But once the medical examiner's office was ready to move the body, they wanted the crowd gone in a hurry."

"Shouldn't we have heard from Heather by now?" Agatha asked. "I'm really worried about her."

"The longer she's there without being charged, the better it is," Coil said. "If she'd said anything incriminating to start with, they'd book her and be on their merry way with yet another bogus arrest."

Hank pulled off his gloves and signaled to the waitress. He could drink a gallon of water on the spot.

"Coil's right," Hank said. "It's a good sign" Hank agreed. "It's also possible they might be holding her as an ace card if Hank really was murdered and they don't have a clue who did it. And I can tell you, there are people at that party who'd be more than happy to see Heather hang for this."

Hank saw the worry in Agatha's eyes, and it ate at his insides that there was nothing more he could do. He put his hand over hers and squeezed gently.

"What did you learn from the bathroom?" Coil asked.

"Lots of gossip and talk about the two gorgeous cops who crashed the party," she said, waving her hand.

"Oh yeah?" Coil asked. "They called us gorgeous?"

Hank's lips twitched as Agatha rolled her eyes.

"The word is," Agatha continued, "that the reason Candy accused Heather was because she was due a sizable settlement upon Buck's death."

"Just Heather?" Coil asked, his cop's eyes going flat. "What about the others?"

"Don't know," Agatha said, shrugging. That's all I heard, and I don't know who was saying it because I was hiding in a stall. Supposedly, Candy suspects Heather because of her track record with huge settlements from past dearly departed husbands."

"Maybe that's what Lorraine was talking about when she said that everything would change now that Buck had truly found the love of his life," Hank said. "Maybe he was cutting them all out of the will."

"Looks like we got some snooping to do," Coil said. "We can find out whether Heather is still a beneficiary on Buck's insurance policies. It's not uncommon for people to forget to change those and end up having an ex-spouse get insurance money."

"Hear anything else?" Coil questioned.

"You mean other than about you?" she asked.

Heat flushed into Coil's cheeks and he tried to look sheepish but failed.

"Those women would eat you up and spit you out, Reggie Coil. Plus, your wife would kill you painfully."

Hank slapped him on the shoulder. "You're too handsome for your own good. You're like an old Brad Pitt, but still, I can see those cowboy good looks somewhere in that weathered face."

"Shut up," Coil said. "You're older than I am. By *a lot*."

"If you two children are finished," Agatha said, "You might be interested to know that word on the street is that Candy was completely blindsided about all the exes showing up. Someone even mentioned maybe Buck was planning to introduce the next potential Mrs. Hazard at the party for everyone to see."

"Only an idiot with a death wish would do that," Hank said, snorting.

"You think Buck had a mistress?" Coil asked.

"I don't know about that," Hank said to Agatha. "I got to talk to his second wife for quite a while before she realized I wasn't assigned to the case. Her name is Lorraine. Seems like a nice lady deep down, and Buck really broke her heart. She said Buck had lured each of them there by being the same old charming man they'd fallen in love with, but Lorraine said Buck told her things were going to change for all of them because he'd found the love of his life in Candy."

Agatha's mouth dropped open. "Buck told her that?"

"That's what she said," Hank said.

"Did he tell her anything else?"

"I don't know," Hank said, mouth twitching slightly. "That's when I got busted and she walked away in a huff. Rich women sure know how to make an exit."

"Well, that stinks," Agatha said, her disappointment obvious. "Do you think Buck was that clueless or that spiteful?"

"Hard to say at this point, but if Buck was murdered it seems like you'd have a pretty good reason to suspect all seven of them."

"Why Candy?" Agatha asked.

"How would you feel if your husband invited all his exes into your home without your knowledge and made hints about changing a will?"

"Oh," Agatha said. "Good point."

"Or maybe the rumor is right, and he really did have a replacement ready to go for number seven."

"We need to tug the inheritance thread," Hank said. "Heather is as much in the dark as we are about why she was there."

"Sex or money," Coil said. "It'll be one of the two."

"Maybe he's been paying all of them in some way all this time," Hank said. "Like an ongoing apology for being such a jerk."

"That could work," Coil said. "He decides to cut them all off, so one of them decides to cut him off."

"I hate to be the bearer of bad news," Agatha said, "But Heather was not receiving a dime from Buck. She got a very nice settlement and some property during the divorce, but she hasn't gotten a cent after that."

"How are you so sure?" Hank asked.

"Heather is as bad with money as she is with men," Agatha said. "I've been her personal bookkeeper for the last ten years. I'd know if Buck was paying her."

Hank looked at Coil and they both grinned.

"So…" Coil asked. "What's she worth?"

"Nunya beeswax," Agatha said.

Chapter Eight

AGATHA WAS IN FOR THE AFTERNOON, AND IT WOULD TAKE
an act of congress to get her to leave the house again. It
was too dang hot.

She'd felt bad for Hank as they'd left the café. He'd
forgotten to cover his seat, and by the way he was scooting
his booty over that padded saddle, she knew it had to be
like sitting on lava. The bike was still new, and he'd eventually remember all the minute details that seemed to go
along with being a motorcycle owner. She hoped.

The air conditioner was set to a chilly sixty-six degrees,
and her shades were drawn so there was no chance of the
sun penetrating. She compensated for the cold interior by
donning her favorite black stretchy pants and an old TCU
t-shirt that she always expected to fall apart every time she
washed it. Her fuzzy socks slipped quietly across the
polished wood floors like a figure skater.

She regretted not making her early morning run, but
the late-night drive from Buck's ranch, and then waiting up
an extra hour in case Heather called, had her plum worn

out. The only reason she'd left the house for lunch was because she hoped Hank and Coil had news, but they hadn't had much.

Agatha slid her way into the home office affectionately called the war room and stretched out on the plush chaise. The war room was one of her favorite places in the old house. She most enjoyed the times she and Hank plotted out crime solving scenarios and book ideas while pouring over old reports and witness statements.

The computer on her desk beeped and she went to check the progress. She'd been downloading the video and pictures Hank had taken of the crime scene. And truth be told, after looking at the scene, she wasn't sure it even was a crime scene. But she knew it had to be worked as a homicide first. Still…there was nothing to suggest it was anything but natural causes.

Buck Hazard was a very powerful man, and it was Detectives Ritzo and Kraken's chance to make themselves relevant. If it was murder, they'd have a huge case on their hands, it would be easy to pin it on Heather. If it was death by natural causes, they'd show that they were diligent in their investigation. Either way, Heather would come out the loser.

She felt her anxiety creep in as she looked at the pictures. She was on a deadline, and she hadn't scheduled Heather going to jail and being accused of murder into her daily writing schedule. This was going to put her way behind. But she'd do whatever she had to do for her friend.

Her computer said she still had twelve minutes to go until everything was uploaded, so she went back to the chaise and dropped down. She could take a twelve-minute nap. It might do her wonders.

She noticed the drawer of the end table was slightly

ajar and she felt the hairs prickle on her scalp. Every once in a while, she'd have a panic attack at the thought of what had happened in that very room only a few months before. It only happened when she was very tired. She could usually control the memories and the panic that came with them.

A breath hitched in her chest, and she sat up quickly and looked in the drawer to make sure her daddy's revolver was still inside. The same revolver she'd used to fatally shoot her stalker, Dr. Ray Salt. Her skin was hot despite the coolness of the room, and she willed herself to lay back down and again and relax. But she remembered all too well how it had felt to fire the revolver, and the bloom of blood across his chest after she'd shot him.

She hadn't told Hank about the panic attacks; sure it was only a matter of time before they faded. But they hadn't. She lay flat on her back on the chaise and held onto each side as the room swayed and she breathed in and out, slow and steady.

She'd tucked her cell phone in the waistband of her stretchy pants, and when it vibrated against her stomach she yelped and rolled off the chaise onto the floor, her breaths coming in shallow pants.

"Get," *pant.* "A grip," *pant.* She stuck her head between her knees and sucked in a couple of deep breaths grabbing the phone. It had stopped ringing, and she saw she'd missed a call from Hank.

It vibrated again in her hand, and she only jumped a little this time.

"Hank," she said, breathing heavy in the phone.

"Agatha?" he asked. "What's wrong? Are you okay?"

"I'm fine," she lied. "Just dozing. The phone scared me. What's up?" She was soaked with sweat, and she put the phone on speaker so she could put her head back between her knees.

"Not much, just wondering if you were able to take a look at the pictures and video from Buck's bedroom," he said.

"You want to come by? I've got everything up on the wall screen."

"I'm actually pulling into your driveway right now," he said. "It was too hot to walk. Of course, the drive is so short the air hasn't even kicked in. Please tell me you have something cold to drink."

"Come on in," she said, frantically trying to look at her appearance in anything that would give a reflection. She used her phone, and then scrubbed her hands over her face to bring some color back into her pale cheeks. Her hair was a mess and damp tendrils stuck to her temples and neck.

She wiped her sweaty palms on her leggings and then skidded her way to the front door. She was a hot mess. Her hands shook as she undid the deadbolt and the chain, and she finally got the door open.

Agatha must've looked worse than she thought because Hank's eyes got big as saucers and his mouth pursed as though he was trying to hold back a yelp of surprise. Which really made her feel bad, considering all the horrific crime scenes he'd looked at over the years.

"Don't ask," she said, and then pulled him inside.

Her lips twitched at his chosen attire. Hank had embraced retirement with full abandon. He wore khaki shorts, and a multicolor Hawaiian shirt that made her eyes cross. He wore his tortoiseshell glasses, which she loved, and a pair of Birkenstocks with white socks. She also knew that he had a weapon strapped somewhere to his body.

"You look…" He looked her up and down from head to toe. "Comfortable," he finally said.

She snorted out a laugh. "Nice save. I've been on the edge of a nap ever since we got home from lunch. My late-night partying days are over. I need a solid eight and my morning run to feel like a human, and I've had neither."

"I can come back later," he said. "You should've told me you needed to rest."

"Nah, if I sleep now it'll throw off my whole schedule," she said. "Besides, I'd hate for you to have gotten dressed up for nothing."

"Hilarious," he said dryly.

She just grinned and headed into the kitchen to get them both an iced tea.

"Lord, it feels good in here," he said. "My windows face the wrong direction and I get all that afternoon sun. My AC is working overtime."

"You need to get the blackout shades like I have. It makes it nice and cozy."

"It mostly makes you a hermit. You have them closed pretty much year-round."

She shrugged, unable to dispute the point, and took the teas into the war room. He'd already made himself comfortable by connecting the computer to her big wall screen.

"Thanks," he said absently, taking the tea from her hand.

"What do you see?" Agatha asked.

"I'd rather not say," he said," I don't want to color any observations you make with what I think."

"Right," Agatha said, squaring her shoulders and looking at the images on screen. She took in every detail, absorbed it and filed it away. She chewed at her bottom lip as she studied, trying to figure out what was bothering her. But she was coming up blank.

"Well, Sherlock?" he asked. "Tell me what you see."

"Well…" Agatha said, and then her phone rang. She looked down at the display and her heart thumped loudly in her chest. She looked up at Hank and said, "It's Heather."

"Saved by the bell."

Chapter Nine

Agatha fumbled with the phone and then said, "Hello? Heather?"

There was silence on the other end.

"Is it her?" Hank asked.

"It's just silence," Agatha said, her frustration obvious.

"Agatha?" Heather said, her voice barely audible through the line.

"Oh, Heather." The relief in her voice couldn't be disguised. "It's me. How are you? Are you okay?"

"I'm sleepy," she said. "And my twenty-four-hour makeup has run out. They don't even have a hair stylist in this place. Can you believe that?"

"Umm…" Agatha said, eyes wide. "Have you had any rest?"

"No," Heather said, yawning, "They said I could sleep in prison. But I met a real cute cop. He brought me something to eat and a Coke. He said they don't have martinis, but you can't convince me there's not a cop in this place who doesn't have a bottle of vodka in their desk drawer."

"Heather, this is serious business," Agatha said. "Aren't you worried?"

"Scared spitless," she said. "But there's nothing I can do as long as these yahoos have an agenda. The dummies are even trying to convince me I actually killed Buck. Which is ridiculous."

"I told you not to talk to those detectives anymore without an attorney present," Agatha said. No one could make her crazy faster than Heather.

"Oh, I know. I figure it's time to call in the big guns. My patience is running thin, and I'm more mad than scared. They caught me off guard last night. I've never actually been arrested, believe it or not, so about halfway to the police station I started thinking this might be a fun little adventure. Like when you do research for your books. And my mugshot looks super cute. Can you call my attorney for me?"

Agatha was speechless for a couple of seconds. "Sure."

"You remember Louise, don't you Agatha?" Heather asked. "She's been with me since my first marriage. I love that woman."

"I'll call her," Agatha said. There were voices in the background, but she couldn't make out what they were saying.

"Cutie Cop says I've gotta go," she said. "He's way nicer than those bozos who brought me in last night. They've been talking me to death, and the one has had a piece of spinach in his teeth since last night. That's disgusting. Talk soon, Agatha. Kisses."

The phone disconnected, and Agatha stared at it like she was in an alternate universe.

"Everything all right?" Hank said tentatively.

"She said there's no hair stylist at the jail and she met a cute cop."

"Sometimes God protects the stupid," Hank said, shaking his head. "Call her attorney and let's get back to work."

Agatha left the room to look up Louise's number. A few minutes later, she felt much better. Louise was a terrifying woman. But they still had an uphill battle. Hank was just hanging up the phone when she came back in the war room.

"Coil said he left another message with the police chief, but he doesn't expect to hear anything back until tomorrow."

"When will the coroner examine Buck's body?" she asked.

"It's doubtful it's a high priority, so I don't see the ME coming in today to do an autopsy. Probably first thing in the morning, and it shouldn't take more than a few hours to get results."

"If it wasn't murder, they'll have to let her go," Agatha said.

"But what if it was?" Hank said, frowning. "I know these guys. They'll charge her for murder before making Buck's COD public just so they can notch an arrest. Once headlines are made, it's easy for people to fall through the cracks.

"What about Nick Dewey?" Agatha asked. "He's got to know the mayor. We're not helpless here. We know people who can help us."

"Good thinking." Hank texted his millionaire friend. They hadn't seen each other since the fire in Rio Chino had killed their police chief, but they stayed in contact by phone. "Done."

"I appreciate it," Agatha said. "I know you don't like having to ask others for help. It means a lot."

Hank brought her in for a hug. "You know you never

have to hesitate to ask me anything. If I can give it to you, I will."

"Which means even more," she said, smiling. "Because you're doing this for Heather, and I know how you feel about her."

"She's an acquired taste," Hank agreed. "But she's growing on me."

Agatha leaned in and kissed him. "I don't do this enough. You're a good man, Hank. I should tell you that more often."

Agatha could see the pleasure in his eyes.

"If you feel like getting out for a bit," he said, "I'll buy you some tea and something sweet from Taco and Waffles."

"You took the words right out of my mouth," she said. "I'll even change clothes first and brush my hair."

"You always look beautiful to me. No need to change."

"That's sweet," she said, smiling. "But it's hot as Hades outside and I'm going to put on shorts and a tank top and put my hair in a ponytail."

She hurried to her bedroom to change and run a brush through her hair, and she caught her reflection in the mirror and grimaced. Her face was still pale from her panic attack, but she'd gotten herself back under control.

She was going to have to do something. There were too many memories in the house. The memories of her parents were sweet, but there were times when an unexpected pang in the heart came out of nowhere. And then there were the memories of Ray Salt, that weren't so sweet.

Agatha jogged back to the front of the house and grabbed her keys from the entry table.

"That was fast," Hank said, eyeing her suspiciously.

"You promised me something sweet," she said. "No reason to dally."

He placed a hand on her arm before she could open the front door. "You okay?"

It was a struggle not to pull away. She'd been alone for so long that she had to get used to trusting someone. And she wasn't altogether comfortable that he could read her so easily.

She let out a slow breath and told him what was on her mind. "I think I'm going to sell the house."

"What?"

"I'm going to sell." Now that she'd said the words aloud, she knew she was going to do it. "It's getting harder and harder to live here."

"Is this about, Salt?" Hank asked.

"This house is a crutch," she said. "I hide here because it's what's easiest for me, but I'm haunted by the memories in it. Ray Salt, my parents, that crazy Santa serial killer, and the daughter I never got a chance to know. I'll never heal as long as I'm tied to this place."

Hank nodded thoughtfully. "Aggie, this is the house your parents built as their home. It wasn't created as a cage for their daughter. Not then or now. If you want to sell it, then put it on the market. But don't let some misplaced sense of obligation steal your joy."

"I've never known anything different," she said. "It's kind of scary."

"It's a frame with paint and shutters. It's rugs and wood floors and drywall. That's all you're selling. You'll make a new home and new memories."

Agatha knew he was right. She'd been born and raised in Rusty Gun. Once her writing career had taken off, she could've easily lived anywhere in the world in any home of her choosing, but at heart, she was a Texan, and her roots were planted deep.

"I'll miss seeing this place. It does have a lot of good memories."

"Actually…" Hank said.

"Actually what?" Agatha asked.

He coughed and pinkened a little.

"I was just thinking that you could see it every day from my house."

"You suggesting something?" Agatha asked, her brows raising.

His color brightened more and a sheen of sweat broke out on his forehead. "I was just thinking I'd love to see you more, but I know how busy you are."

"You are so bad at talking about feelings," she said, shaking her head, but there was a smile on her lips. And then she chuckled.

"I don't want to say the wrong thing. This is new territory for me. It's been a really long time since I even thought about…" he made a motion with his hands back and forth to encompass both of them.

He took a deep breath and blurted out the words. "I'm just saying, if you want to hang out at my place, you're always welcome."

"Hang out or move in?" she asked, cocking a hand on her hip.

He swallowed hard, and he seemed to pale. "Is that what you want?"

"Oh, no. Don't deflect this. You started this so you've got to have the guts to finish it."

He gaped at her a few seconds with his mouth opening and closing, but no words came out. She smiled and patted him on the chest and then moved to open the door. Hank was still standing in the house like a fish out of water when she turned back to look at him.

"Let's go," she said, feeling much lighter of heart. "I want churros."

Chapter Ten

HANK FELT LIKE HE WAS HOLDING A GRENADE WITHOUT THE pin in it. He had no idea what had happened or how things had spiraled out of control. In his mind, he knew exactly what he wanted. It was just his mouth that didn't know how to get the words out.

He'd thought at the very least Agatha would be upset or offended in some way, but she'd just smiled at him and they'd gone on to Taco and Waffles like nothing had happened. He knew how her mind worked, and he knew if he wanted the end results he kept seeing in his mind, then his mouth was going to have to start talking sooner rather than later.

Despite his stumbling, they had a nice time out, and both of them were more relaxed when they got back to Agatha's house.

"Nick left a message while we were driving," Hank said once they'd gotten out of the heat. "Let me give him a call, and I'll get things set up in the war room so we can get back to business."

The war room inside of Agatha's home was Hank's

favorite space to work. She'd set it up as a place where she buried herself beneath the mountains of investigations she used to write her bestselling crime novels. The technology and in-house resources she had were more efficient than most police departments.

"Sounds good, roomie," Agatha said. "I'm going to change back into my comfy clothes."

"Roomie?" Hank said, watching her disappear down the hallway.

When she came back, she was dressed in her habitual work uniform of leggings, a t-shirt, and socks. Agatha was definitely a creature of habit.

"Nick's texts said he'd call the mayor, and he asked for a status on whether Heather had representation. I let him know that she'd have someone there today."

"Nick's calling the mayor on a Sunday?" Agatha asked.

"They're very good friends."

"Thanks. I guess we're going to owe him one," she said. "Why's it so hard getting answers from people? Kraken and Ritzo aren't autonomous. This is Dallas PD for Pete's sake, not Podunk nowhere."

"It's common in high-profile deaths," Hank said. "The best way to appease all the bankers, lawyers, and media asking questions is to investigate and yank in a suspect. Politics sucks."

"No kidding," she agreed.

Agatha turned on her wall screen and went to work on her computer. They worked in silence for more than an hour before her head came up and her eyes focused on him.

"I've been digging into the clerk of courts office, and I've managed to find insurance records and divorce decrees. Wives are an expensive business."

"Not really," Hank said. "It's when they become ex-wives that things get expensive. Longevity is key."

"I'll remember that," she said. "Maybe you should look over these. There's a lot of legalese you might be more familiar with."

"Okay."

"Just take my seat," she said. "I want to look at the scene again anyway."

He grabbed a legal pad and pen and started wading through the muck, making notes and matching up names and settlements. He connected companies, mergers, stocks, bonds, and properties hidden in different LLCs. There were properties and accounts he'd opened in his children's names, two of which were still minors.

He'd traced multiple filings on behalf of *Grace, Strong, Olivia, Sanderson and* Saul, which appeared to be a very exclusive law firm. They'd filed wills, trusts, estate plans and insurance proclamations on behalf of Buck Hazard for almost fifty years, and they'd also dealt with numerous lawsuits that had come during the course of his business.

Hank refocused his efforts on the law firm. There was a loose thread somewhere that he could use to unravel the past, and hopefully protect Heather's future. He started with the easiest searches in social media. Other than the firm's presence on a few sites and a very stoic website, there wasn't much to be gained. Everyone in the firm was close to, if not the same age, as Buck, and there were no red flags from the Texas Bar Association's records. All looked to be in legitimate working order.

Hank did notice that the firm was incorporated about the same time that Buck's company, Texas Hazard, Co began to launch. It was possible that one of the law partners was a friend or classmate to Buck. Maybe their relationship grew from friends to professional and Buck trusted that one person. But which one?

"How's it going?"

"Very interesting," Hank said. "You?"

"I don't know," she said, thoughtfully. "But something about the scene is bothering me. I figure my brain will put it together at some point, but for now it's like a bunch of puzzle pieces are floating around in my brain and not fitting together."

Hank understood her frustration. There were so many times he'd stood over a dead body and allowed distractions to vacate his mind. Then he'd allow the scene to speak to him. He didn't want anyone else's opinion or report at that moment. Some of the detectives called him the death whisperer, but he accepted it as a compliment. He had a calling to learn the victims, to understand them, empathize with them, and ultimately, bring them justice.

The law firm was definitely making his Spidey-senses tingle. Sometimes it wasn't as much about what was in the file as much as it was who prepared it. Hank was so close to finding out the who and knew that would satisfy his why. He clicked back on the law firm's website. There was an old picture of the five partners sitting around a massive table. It wasn't the warmest or most welcoming photo he'd ever seen, but he assumed they were good at what they did. Men like Buck didn't become successful because they surrounded themselves with stupid people.

Hank kept the page's URL open in a separate tab before he returned to the clerk of court's website to dig deeper. But his gaze kept veering back to the four men and one woman in the picture.

"That's it," he said, his palms slapping the desktop.

Agatha jumped a foot and put her hand over her heart. "What's it?" she asked.

"I think I figured out what thread to pull."

"Want to share?" she asked.

"Not yet. Let me put some things together and make it organized first."

"Okay," she agreed. "When you take a break, I think I might need to talk some of these photos out loud. Though I really did enjoy the video of you sneezing all over the camera. Remind me to Clorox my phone."

Hank felt the heat rise to his cheeks. "Sorry about that. There was one of those scent vapor machines going strong, but it was worse because it was covering up some strong perfume. My sinuses were getting an overload."

He arched a brow in that way he thought was cute, and he felt his heart turn over in his chest. He had it bad. And he really needed to get his mouth in tune with his brain so he could tell her how he felt.

"Give me a few more minutes with this, and then you can talk out the scene," he said.

He refocused on the picture. It couldn't have been easy to become a partner in a law firm like this one, and by the looks of them, he wouldn't want to come across any of them in a courtroom unless they were on his side.

By the age of the picture, he assumed it would've been almost impossible for the lone woman to have broken the ranks a few decades ago. What sealed the deal for Hank was the positioning of everyone in the picture. Either they wanted to highlight that a female was a partner, or they wanted nothing to do with her. Hank guessed the latter. Now he had to figure out who she was and why she was the outcast.

"Ava Sanderson," he said. She would lead him to answers. His gut stirred every time he looked at her. He did a Google and social media search on her and came up with nothing. Not even one hit. But there she was, in the good old Texas Department of Motor Vehicles. Ava Sanderson was actually Ava Hazard Sanderson. It wasn't long before social security and birth records showed him that Ava was not another one of Buck's ex-wives. She was his sister.

Seems Ava was a graduate of the University of Texas School of Law and passed the bar on her first take. He figured she, like most new lawyers, would've served as a clerk for a judge until she was able to secure a job as an associate with a firm. She got her feet wet for a year, and was named senior partner with *Grace, Strong, Olivia, Sanderson and Saul*. Of course, she was the Sanderson.

"Nothing fishy there," he muttered.

Hank continued to make notes of the timeline, and he could make a very educated guess that she used her brother and his millions of dollars as leverage to up her position in the firm. Up until that time, their client list was steady, but hardly of the caliber that Buck would bring them. And as luck would have it, Ava lived exactly halfway between Rusty Gun and Dallas. It was Sunday, and a good time to do a cold call on a hot lead.

"I think we need to make a trip," he said.

"I can't eat anymore churros," she said. "Besides, my stomach is in a knot right now."

Hank removed his reading glasses and rubbed his eyes. They'd been at it for a while. He looked at the online news source she had on the projection screen and he winced. Heather's face was the image for the leading story—*Texas Socialite Dragged In For Murder Of Local Philanthropist.*"

Hank whistled and put his arm around her waist. "I'm sorry, Aggie."

"Why couldn't they use her mugshot for the front page?"

"Huh?" Hank was thoroughly confused.

"Look," she said, pointing to the screen. "They used a

picture from when Heather fell into the fountain. See, I'm trying to pull her out."

"It's not a terrible picture," Hank said, squinting his eyes. "It looks kind of…frolicking. Was Heather drunk?"

"Yes." She stared at him long and hard. "Put your glasses on and tell me what you see."

He did as she asked and then gasped. Heather looked like she was on the cover of a magazine, her drunken smile infectious, and her bright green dress eye-catching as she kicked water at Agatha.

Agatha, on the other hand, looked like a drowned rat, and her dress was up over her backside so her very nice black underwear was exposed to the picture taker.

"Oh," he said. "Nice panties."

"Shut up."

Chapter Eleven

"I THINK I'VE NAILED DOWN WHAT'S BEEN RATTLING around my brain," Agatha said.

"I thought I smelled something burning," he said, chuckling.

"You're just a laugh riot today," she said.

"I think you're a bad influence on me."

She grinned and turned back to the pictures she'd put back up on the screen. "I want to talk this through, but tell me if you've already thought of any of these things."

"Will do."

Agatha had switched to water because she could feel her system start to jolt with all the tea in her system.

"Buck was found resting on his right side as though he'd been sleeping," she said. "But look what's noticeable once I blew up the photos and lightened them a bit."

Hank nodded, proud of her for seeing what he'd noticed earlier. He'd said it before, but she would've made a dang good cop.

"There are signs of lividity in his left calf, hamstring, triceps and neck." She moved to the next enhanced photo

LILIANA HART & LOUIS SCOTT

and grinned. "But look at the right arm. There are signs of lividity in the arm, but not in the triceps. The coloring is on the outside of the arm, which means he didn't die laying on his right side like the picture shows. You can also see the lividity on the bottom of his feet."

"The body always tells a story," Hank said.

Agatha nodded. "So, when Buck died, he was sitting up on the side of the bed, feet on the floor. He dies and falls back onto the bed." She demonstrated on the chaise. "His left arm was next to his body, but the right arm was extended. Almost as if it were reaching for something."

Hank rocked back on his heels and stuck his hands in the pockets of his cargo shorts. She was good. Very good.

"The drawer is open on the nightstand," he said. "Maybe that's what he was reaching for."

"A gun?" she asked. "I didn't see any pictures of what was inside the drawer."

"Our time was limited, and I didn't notice the drawer was open until I started examining the photos."

"Could be anything in there," she said. "And maybe he wasn't reaching for anything at all. It takes about half an hour for lividity to set in, but to get that level of deep purple you're looking between an hour or two that he was in that position after death. So, he was definitely moved a while after he died."

"Do you think Heather touched him when she went in to meet him?" Hank asked.

Agatha shrugged. "She said no, but you never know."

"Nice work, Sherlock. So how does this line up with time of death, and who had access to him?"

"Heather and I went into check the room just after nine o'clock. It was still light outside, but it would've been full dark in another half hour. From the time Heather disappeared from the conversation we were having to when she came out screaming was between five and ten minutes. I sent you a text when she ditched me."

Agatha got out her cell phone and checked the text log. "So, Heather went off at eight-fifty. Then if you work backward from that, based on the color of lividity, you're looking at a TOD between six-fifty and seven forty-five. I added a few minutes in both directions."

"What time did guests start arriving?" Hank asked.

"The invitation said guests could arrive at noon for horseback rides, skeet shooting, or swimming. Box lunches would be provided. The open bar started serving at three, so my guess is that most of the guests began arriving after that time. Heather and I arrived around six because it took her two hours to pick just the right outfit and get her hair and makeup done, so it made us late."

"You saw Buck when you arrived?" Hank asked.

"Yeah, he was there to greet us. He kissed Heather on the cheek and whispered something in her ear that had her giggling. I'd already seen the margarita machines, so I headed in that direction while she was getting reacquainted."

"You said Heather got a text from Buck telling her to meet him in the bedroom?"

"Oh," she said, the light dawning. "She got that text right before she found him. Buck would've already been dead."

"Bingo," he said. "So somewhere between seven forty-five and the time Heather found him an hour later, someone came in and moved the body."

"The killer? Why would they do that?"

"Either the killer or someone else who happened to stumble upon him. Maybe they thought he was asleep and tried to wake him up, and then once they realized he was dead they were too afraid to speak up."

Agatha went to her white board and started writing down the timeline, from when guests started arriving to when she and Heather walked in on the body. She always did better with visuals.

"That sure doesn't leave a lot of time for the killer," Agatha said, tapping the end of the marker against her chin.

"The good thing about a tight time for opportunity is that it eliminates so many other possibilities.," Hank said.

"All we need to do is find out who arrived at what time, and that's our suspect pool," she said.

"According to Lorraine," Hank said, and then added, "She's ex-wife number two."

"Right."

"She said Hank sent a car for her to the airport and she arrived right at five o'clock."

"Okay," she said, adding Lorraine's name to the time-line. "Of course, there's still the possibility this wasn't murder, and this is a complete waste of our time. But I'm not willing to bet Heather's future against that. You'd think the M.E. would make an exception and get started early considering Buck is practically considered a state treasure. He was friends with Ross Perot for Pete's sake."

"It's a long holiday weekend," Hank reminded her, "We'll be lucky if it's not some intern catching corpses until everyone gets back from vacation."

Agatha pressed her lips together. It wasn't often she thought about where she might be now if she'd been able to continue with her original dream of forensics. Dr. Salt had changed the whole course of her future. But if he hadn't, she never would've met Hank. And she probably wouldn't be a writer.

She shook herself out of it and said, "One of his shoes was kicked under the bed."

"Yeah, I noticed that right off. It seemed off to me then, and it still does now." He scratched his head a bit. Agatha grinned as she wondered how many times he'd done just that while working high-risk investigations with the FBI. She knew he wasn't looking at what was on the screen as much as he was exploring what wasn't on there.

"Let's walk it out. The man is hosting a party with a couple hundred guests. He's got big plans for the evening that somehow involve each of his exes. He moves to his private suite, expecting to conduct his meetings there. Seems a little presumptuous to be in the bedroom instead of the office, but from what I can tell, Buck liked to play with his prey before he cut them off at the knees.

"For whatever reason, he sits on the edge of the bed. Maybe he got into an argument and got winded. He's still a seventy-six-year old man. He's wearing his sandals because he's been back and forth between his suite of rooms and the patio and pool area. If he's in distress, the last thing you're thinking of is taking your shoes off. One of them is lined up neatly next to the bed, but the other got kicked, either by Buck as he was struggling, or by someone else."

"And the someone else would've had to have been up close and personal," Agatha said.

"I didn't see any ligature marks or bruising around the neck," Hank said.

"No," she said, rubbing her eyes. "I think I need a break."

"Good idea," Hank said, looking at his watch. "Remember how I said we needed to take a road trip?"

"I thought that was for more churros," Agatha said.

"No, I found something interesting while going through all the reports. You should be a P.I. You have a scary amount of access into people's lives."

She smiled and shrugged. "You pay the subscription fees, you can have access to almost anything."

"As a cop, that's terrifying. But anyway, I discovered that Buck's sister is also his attorney. I sent her an email with my credentials and told her I had doubts to the competence of the detectives working her brother's case. I asked if she'd mind if we talked to her."

"Wow," Agatha said, brows raising. "I never would've had the guts to cold call someone like that, especially the victim's sister."

"The worst she can do is say no," he said.

"I'm assuming you need to stop by your house and change clothes?" she asked.

"Why would you assume that?"

Agatha's mouth pressed in a thin line, but she wasn't quite sure how to answer tactfully.

"Just kidding," he said. "Of course I'm going to change. I suggest you do the same."

"I won't judge your retirement clothes if you won't judge my work clothes," she said.

"Speaking of work clothes," he said. "I noticed you've added a piece of jewelry to your ensemble. I never took you for the rubber bracelet kind of woman. I've been trying to subtly read what it says all day, but I haven't been able to manage it."

Agatha looked down at her wrist to the red rubber bracelet that still sat there. "Oh," she said. "I completely forgot I was wearing it."

She started to take it off, but then she thought of something. "Hank. These bracelets were given to all the invited guests. They were given to us at a checkpoint gate about half a mile from the main driveway. I was Heather's plus one, and she had to give my name with the RSVP weeks ago.

"After they gave us the bracelets, they directed us to a parking area, and then we had to scan our bracelets on some kind of electric turn style. It was kind of like going to Disney World.

As soon as we scanned the bracelets our names came up. This is how we can get a guest list."

"So, what does it say?" he asked.

"It says, "Have a Buckin' Good Time.""

Chapter Twelve

"ARE WE THERE YET?" AGATHA ASKED WITH A CHEEKY grin.

He'd never seen so many twenty-file mile an hour speed zones. They'd been in the same neighborhood for what felt like a hundred years.

"Good Lord," he said as he had to slow down to a crawl to drive over a speed hump. "I've never seen a neighborhood so concerned with speeders. You could get out of the car and run to her house before I get there."

"I've already considered that option," Agatha said. "I had to go to the bathroom three speed humps ago."

He grunted and kept driving.

"Did you read that article about Heather in the paper?" she asked.

"The one showing the world your skivvies?"

"Yes," she said dryly. "Thanks for reminding me."

"Then, no. I didn't read it. I was too distracted by the picture."

"Well, whoever that dumb reporter was interviewed Buck's poor, grieving widow. You'd think she was working the case with as much speculation as she cast on Heather. As far as she's concerned, Heather is guilty as sin and she doesn't care if they're able to prove it with actual evidence."

"She must've gone to detective school with Ritzo and Kraken," Hank said.

"Candy said that Heather has motive because she's supposed to inherit a ton of money when Buck dies, and that Buck was going to change his will. She said Heather must've found out about it and that's why she killed him."

Hank whistled. "That certainly doesn't sound like good news for the home team. If Candy can make Heather the bad guy, it won't matter if she's innocent. The entire city will convict her of murder."

"Then step on it," she said. "I don't care if you've got to drive on people's lawns to get around these things. Buck's sister is older than he is. She could die before we get there."

Hank chuckled and noticed the farther they drove through the neighborhood the nicer the houses. The lawns took up half a block, and then the full block, and the houses were like castles.

"Holy cow," Hank said. "No wonder they've got all those speed humps. They don't want anyone coming back here. What kind of people live in houses like these?"

"Rich people," Agatha said. "You met a bunch of them last night."

Hank grunted. "That's her house at the end of the road with the gate facing us."

"It feels like we're being watched," she said. "This place gives me the creeps."

"We are being watched. I've seen cameras in trees every twenty-five feet or so, and there are cameras at every gate we drive past.

Hank pulled up to the ornate iron gate and rolled down his window so he could press the call button.

"May I help you," a cultured voice said.

"Hank Davidson to see Mrs. Sanderson. She's expecting me."

"Please drive through. You may park your car under the covered area."

Hank rolled up the window and Agatha waggled her eyebrows. "Fancy. I wonder if he wears a tuxedo and carries around a silver tray."

"Why would he carry around a silver tray?" Hank asked.

"I don't know. It just seems like something a butler should carry."

The massive gate slid open and Hank drove through. There were beautiful trees and flower beds artfully displayed in the yard, a white sweetheart swing that hung from a tree, and a pair of cannons.

"The cannons are an interesting touch," Agatha said. "She probably used them during the Civil War to protect her property."

Hank's shoulders shook with laughter. Agatha could always make him laugh.

The house finally came into view and they weren't disappointed. It was just...big. Hank had no idea what style it was, and he didn't particularly care, but it screamed money more ostentatiously than Buck's ranch.

"No accounting for taste I guess," Agatha said.

Hank smiled and scanned the property as he looked for the covered parking area. The driveway in front of the house was a huge semi-circle, but the driveway continued on the opposite side and led around to the side of the house. That's when Hank saw the covered parking area.

"I guess she didn't want my car to be seen from the

street," Hank said. He backed into the parking spot and left the car running and in drive for the time being.

"It's a BMW," Agatha said. "Why wouldn't she want that to be seen?"

"Maybe because it's not a Bentley. I have a feeling a BMW would be slumming for Mrs. Sanderson."

Leaving the car in drive was a common practice that cops learned on the job. Just in case they had to escape an ambush or chase a fleeing suspect.

Hank noticed a curtain move next to the side door. Then something out of his periphery had him looking at the other end of the house, where another curtain moved.

"Keep an eye on that last window in the corner of the house," Hank said.

"They're watching us," she said. "I saw two curtains move. You think this is a trap?"

"Not sure, but she might just be taking precautions because she thinks her brother was murdered."

"Do you know if she lives with anyone but the butler?"

"I was under the impression she lived alone, so I can't be sure who else is in there besides the two of them."

The door on the side of the house was nice enough to be on the front of the house, and it finally opened to reveal a scarecrow of a man with a sharp pointed nose and thinning silver hair. He was dressed in black trousers, a black vest, and a white, long sleeve button-down shirt.

"Man, I can't believe he's not holding a silver tray," Agatha said. "I'm so disappointed."

Hank put the car in park and turned off the ignition. And then he and Agatha got out of the car slowly.

"Hello," Hank said. "I'm Hank Davidson. I emailed Mrs. Sanderson about asking questions regarding the death of her brother."

He nodded once and said, "She'll speak with you in the parlor. Come inside."

Hank kept vigilant watch as they approached the house, and he tapped his elbow against the pistol at his waist. It was a reassurance, just to make sure it was there if he needed it. He'd put on a light sport coat to conceal the weapon.

"You have identification?" the butler asked.

Technically, Hank was walking a very shaky line. He had a badge, but he was retired, though there were still privileges with that designation that regular civilians didn't have. He took his commission out of his back pocket and showed it to the butler. Like most people, he glanced at it briefly and nodded.

"I'm Stewart," he said. "Mrs. Sanderson's majordomo. If you need anything, you only have to alert me."

"We appreciate the time, Stewart," Agatha said, giving him a smile. It didn't make a dent in his rigid personality.

They walked in to a spacious kitchen with rich woods and copper accents and followed Stewart through several rooms that looked overstuffed and unused until they finally reached what Hank assumed was the parlor.

Hank blinked a couple of times when they walked into the room. It was impossibly white—carpet, walls, and furniture. Even the cat was white.

Ava Sanderson sat in a chair that looked like a throne. She was formidable, even at an advanced age, though she didn't look to be a woman in her eighties. She could've passed for twenty years younger. Her spine was straight as a rod, and her white hair was short and ruthlessly tamed behind her ears. She wore silver loungewear, and Hank wondered how many people relaxed at home on a Sunday wearing their pearls.

"Detective," Mrs. Sanderson said. "I didn't realize you were bringing a guest."

"Agatha Harley," Agatha said, nodding to her. "Pleasure to meet you."

Hank was glad they'd both taken the time to dress a little nicer. Agatha wore black slacks and a sleeveless poppy colored shell, and she'd put her hair up in a loose bun on top of her head and a few strands of dark hair framed her face.

"We want to offer our condolences on your brother's passing," Agatha said.

Ava Sanderson seemed to deflate a little at the mention of her brother's death. "I appreciate that," she said softly. "It's been hard to come to grips with." Mrs. Sanderson turned to Stewart. "Bring iced tea into the living room. It's too darned hot for anything else."

Hank's brows raised. She'd relaxed her guard enough for her accent to slip through, and he wondered if there was more to her than there seemed.

"Y'all might as well have a seat," she said. "No reason standing there gawking at me. I wanted to check you out good and proper. A lady my age can't be too careful. I did a Google search on you after you emailed Detective Davidson. You have a very impressive record."

"Thank you, ma'am."

"No need to ma'am me," she said. "Just call me Ava. Well, come on." She got up from the throne chair and went to a door on the opposite side of the room. "I hate this room, but all those rich yahoos seem to like it. We'll be much more comfortable in here."

Ava opened the door to a small, comfortable room decorated in soft blues.

"The front part of the house is for guests and parties," she said. "Though I don't give them as much as I used to. I have an image to maintain, and people in my circles are very unforgiving if you slip in the maintenance."

"It sounds like more trouble than it's worth," Hank said.

She gave him a soft smile, and her eyes crinkled. "Quite right. Now sit down and Stewart will bring in some tea and cookies."

Hank and Agatha sat on an overstuffed sofa, and Ava took the matching chair next to him.

"You're an interesting woman, Ava," Hank said.

"Oh, you have to be if you get to be my age," she said. "Did you know there were no other women in my graduating class when I was in law school? We started with sixty-three women. And I was the only one who made it to the end. I'm just as stubborn and hardheaded as Buck. And I know how to fight and get what I want. We get it honest. I still have clients. I think the day I stop working is the day I'll die. It keeps me going. I'm twelve years older than my brother. Did you know that?"

"I did," he admitted.

She nodded as if she were proud of him for checking her out. "Time's slipping away from me. I should have gone before Buck, but he lived fast and hard. He was on borrowed time."

"How so?" Hank asked.

"Buck tried his best to cling to his youth by marrying younger women. He's always been a bit insecure. Even as a child. He was somewhat of a surprise for my parents. They thought they were through with having children when he came along. They were both in their forties, and I think Buck felt their exhaustion at having a young child at that point in their lives. People in their forties back then were considered ancient compared to today. My mother was actually quite embarrassed to find herself in the family way. Their feelings made Buck feel like he was unwanted, and I think that always stuck with him."

Stewart picked that moment to come back in with a cart that held three glasses of sweet tea and a plate of cookies that were so perfect they looked like they came out of a magazine. Everything was arranged on a silver tray.

Hank looked over at Agatha and saw she was biting her lip to keep from grinning, and she waggled her eyebrows at him.

"It's sad," Ava said. "Each of his wives was young, but none of them were the fountain of youth he was looking for. He would've been better off seeing his doctor once every few years instead of having another wedding."

"Did he have health problems?" Agatha asked, taking one of the cookies and a napkin.

Hank took a cookie of his own and a glass of sweet tea, and he set it on the coaster on the little table next to him before biting into the cookie. His eyes closed in pure pleasure as the soft, butter cookie all but melted in his mouth.

"He had heart issues the last five years, but nothing a little exercise and diet wouldn't have fixed. But Buck was stubborn as a mule and wouldn't listen to reason. He had an answer for everything. That's why he always married a nurse. That way he always had someone to take care of him."

"Is that so?" Hank asked, catching Agatha's eye so she'd remain silent. He could tell she wanted to say something about Heather. "All of his wives were nurses?"

"Except for one." She tapped a manicured nail against her chin. "I can't recall which one. It was one of them in the middle."

"Heather Cartwright?" Agatha asked.

Ava snapped her fingers. "That's the one."

"Why'd Buck marry her if she wasn't a nurse?" Agatha asked.

"It was impossible to know all the thoughts in Buck's head. But honestly, I think he loved her. He always said she couldn't help his heart, but she could help heal it."

"Did you know that the police suspect Heather in your brother's death?" Hank asked. "It seems Candy was able to be very persuasive in her arguments to the detectives in charge of the case and to the media."

"I've tried to keep up," she said, mouth pursing tightly. "And I've had dealings through the years with the detectives in charge. Morons. Spiteful, vengeful men who are a disgrace to the badge."

"We can agree on that a hundred percent," Hank said.

"I've kept my mouth shut for decades about Buck's wives and the life he led," she continued. "Honestly, I think he spent his life looking for the love he never had as a child. I won't call those women gold diggers because he pursued them for specific reasons too. They all fit a profile. But he was different with Heather. She wasn't just another woman. They tried to have children, but she wasn't able. It was heartbreaking for both of them. I think that was the straw that broke their marriage, and believe me there were a lot of straws. But he didn't stop loving her."

"What kind of straws?" Agatha asked.

"Money meant nothing to Buck. He made some, lost some, and then made a bunch. He spent lavishly, and he took care of his friends or people closest to him. Including his ex-wives. He figured money was a good apology for being married to him. When each of his marriages ended, he kept them all on payroll on a quarterly retainer. It wasn't a fortune when you look at his income, but it was enough for each of those women to live comfortably. Except for Heather. When they divorced, she refused the monthly settlement. She wanted a clean break. I think that hurt him more than anything.

"But Buck had the last laugh. She didn't accept the quarterly payments, but he made her the beneficiary in his will. The kids would inherit the business and several investments. But the bulk of his estate would go to Heather. I know the details because I drew up his will."

"Did he plan on paying them indefinitely?" Agatha asked.

Her smile was sly, and there was a twinkle in her pale blue eyes. "No," she said. "In fact, Buck was planning on dropping quite the bombshell on each of them. It seems little Candy has vicious claws, and she was tired of him having any connection, especially a financial connection, with the women of his past. She gave him an ultimatum."

"Did she know Heather was included in Buck's will?" Hank asked.

"She did," Ava said. "And I have no idea how she found out. The only person who has ever known the contents of Buck's will for the past fifty years is Buck and me. I've made the adjustments that need to be made through the year, but the contents have always been sealed. And I don't believe my brother would've shared them with Candy. He never shared that information with any of his wives."

"What'd she do when she found out?" Agatha asked.

"It wasn't pretty," Ava said, and there was a gleeful look in her eyes as she recounted the event. "She was mad as a hornet when she came storming into my office. She called me all kinds of vile names and demanded that I immediately remove Heather's name from "Our will" as she kept calling it. She tried to insinuate that Buck was too old to make decisions of this magnitude, and she was going to press for diminished capacity.

"I told her she was crazy as a bedbug, and then she really got mad. She told me it was my fault and that she was going to complain to the bar association for giving advice to a client that wasn't in his best interest, and that I was no longer competent to practice law. I enjoyed her show of temper for about ten or fifteen minutes, at least until she started breaking things, and then I told her to get out. I have to admit I would've liked to have popped her one right in her nose job. She told me, rather dramatically I might add, that I was going to be sorry. And then she stormed out and slammed the door behind her."

"She actually threatened you?" Agatha asked. She reached out and touched Ava's hand sympathetically.

Hank noticed the move and was happy that he and Agatha worked so well together. He had highly trained partners in the past that had failed to read the situation while questioning someone. But he knew that Agatha anticipated the conversation was moving closer to attorney/client privilege and confidentiality expectations. Making that personal contact was a great move for helping to ease Ava into more details.

"She sure did, but she doesn't scare me. I was on the team that helped put Happy Clarke in prison back in nineteen sixty-seven. Candy hasn't got anything on the mafia when it comes to intimidation tactics."

"Wow," Agatha said. "I'd love to hear all of that story one day."

"Any time," she said.

"What do you think happened to Buck?" Hank asked. "He could've died from natural causes."

"Fiddlesticks," she said. "Buck had just had a physical and a checkup. "I told him inviting all those women to the party was a mistake, but he just laughed and said it would be great entertainment. Even better than the fireworks. He was murdered. No doubt in my mind. The question is, who did it?"

"I don't suppose we could get the particulars of the will where Heather is concerned?" Agatha asked.

"You're a friend of Heather's?" Ava asked, shrewdly.

"She's my best friend. And she's been sitting in jail since last night. If Ritzo and Kraken can do it, she'll end up taking the fall for Buck's murder."

"Oh, they can do it," she said. "I've seen it happen. Which is why I knew your name was familiar," she said, looking at Hank. "I know you've donated a lot of your time to the Innocence Project."

"Yes," he said. "But this time I'm going to take them down. They've tarnished the badge for too long."

"Well then," she said, clasping her hands together. "I don't see why I can't give you a copy of the will, considering Heather is the beneficiary. We'll call you her representatives to make it a little less sticky since she's in jail. I've been an attorney a long time, but I never allowed myself to get jaded by the system or bilk my clients for money for no reason. I believe in justice. I'll send a copy of the will to your email."

"We appreciate it," Hank said.

"You don't happen to have that cookie recipe," Agatha said, eating the crumbs off her napkin. They'd managed to finish off all of the cookies during their conversation.

"The will I'll give you," Ava said. "But the cookie recipe is a family secret."

"Understood," Agatha said. "May I use your bathroom before we go? I can't make it past the speed humps again."

"If you go fast enough you barely even feel them," Ava said. "The bathroom is through that door there."

They said their goodbyes a few minutes later, and Stewart showed them back out the side door.

Agatha waited until they were in the car before she asked, "What do you think?"

"It's hard not to like a woman who's gone toe to toe with one of the most infamous mobsters in the country."

"I want to be like her when I grow up," Agatha said, settling back for the drive to Rusty Gun.

Chapter Thirteen

"WE'RE CLOSER TO CANDY'S HOME THAN WE ARE TO ours," Agatha said to Hank. "Why don't we drop by and see if she'll talk to us? She hasn't shut up to anyone who would listen since Buck died. Maybe she'll give us the same courtesy."

"Maybe," Hank agreed. "I doubt she's home though. And how in the heck are we supposed to get in? They've probably still got the crime scene tape up."

Agatha held her arm up and so the red rubber bracelet could be seen on her arm. With the chaos following Buck's death, I bet they haven't dismantled the entrance point for the party."

"Hmm," Hank said.

Agatha smiled as she recognized the sound Hank made whenever he was thinking through scenarios. But his interest was piqued.

Instead of taking the exit that would've led them back to Rusty Gun, he took the exit leading them toward Dallas.

"Coil texted while we were talking to Ava," Agatha said. "I reached out to him earlier to see what he could find out about the bracelets and the guest list. I read off the brand name on the bracelet, and Coil said he knew the guy who owned the company. Someone name Joel."

"Well, that's great news."

"Kind of," she said. "Apparently it's not a problem for the guy to access the data, but the collection device is still at the party."

"Maybe we can borrow it if we manage to get on the property."

"Borrow it?" Agatha said, grinning. "Why Hank Davidson, I think I've become a bad influence on you."

He just grunted and kept his eyes on the road, but she could've sworn she saw his mouth twitch.

"I still don't understand why Ritzo and Kraken would focus in on Heather when all the ex-wives were on the property," she said. "They didn't even consider talking to them."

"Seriously?" Hank asked. "Heather is going to inherit a whole bunch of money. And Candy knew it. That gives Heather means, motive, and opportunity."

"Would Heather lose the inheritance if she was arrested for murder?" Agatha asked.

"It could certainly be contested and tied up in the courts," Hank said. "And if she were found guilty, she could lose it."

It was an hour and a half drive to Dallas, and it would be dark by the time they got there. Probably a good thing since their being on the property wasn't exactly above board. She laid her seat back and closed her eyes, while Hank put in his ear buds and listened to his latest A.C. Riddle mystery on audiobook.

Hank turned his headlights off as they turned onto the long road that led to Buck's ranch. It was a private road, so there was no traffic. There were a couple of trucks parked in the field where they'd set up games and the fireworks, but other than that, there didn't seem to be anyone else around.

"What about the staff?" Agatha asked. "Maybe we should knock on the door, just in case."

"We can," Hank said while reaching for a red-lens flashlight to help from being detected. "But I think that would get us scooted out of here in a hurry. Let's just see what we see."

"I didn't exactly dress for B and E," she said, looking down at her shirt and ballet flats."

"I've got a go-bag in the trunk," Hank said. "I think I've got a black jacket in there."

Agatha met Hank at his open trunk, and he was digging into a black bag. He pulled out a black long sleeve shirt and pulled it on over his white dress shirt and weapon. Then he handed her a black Gortex jacket that was several sizes too large, but it's not like she could expect him to carry her size in the trunk of his car.

She put it on and zipped it up, and then rolled up the sleeves so they didn't hang down past her hands.

"There are going to be motion-activated perimeter lights all around," Hank said, "So we can either try to avoid them, or just go ahead and let them pop on. It's not unusual for these kinds of lights to get activated, so I wouldn't particularly worry about it. Any number of things could set them off, from wild animals to a strong gust of wind."

They moved quickly down the half mile path toward the house and the scanner that was set up to open the gate so they could get onto the property.

"Looks like I'm getting my run in today anyway," she said, panting as they approached the gates.

Her adrenaline was pumping, and she was more out of

breath than she should've been because of it. Her hands were sweaty, and she wiped her palms on her slacks. It was just now starting to dawn on her what they were about to do.

"Oh, man," she said.

"Second thoughts?" Hank whispered.

She shook her head and then realized Hank probably couldn't see her, so she said, "No."

She reminded herself that Heather was worth breaking and entering for. Though it wouldn't do Heather a whole lot of good if she was occupying the cell next to her.

They approached the gate and the box where she could scan her bracelet.

"Wait," she said, pulling her arm back before the chip could be scanned.

"What?" Hank asked.

"This will show that I was here tonight. How in the world will I explain that?"

"We're taking the box when we leave, and in the slight chance of the data being stored in a cloud, just tell whoever asks that the bracelet fell off at the party."

"Wow," she said dryly. "You had that one ready to go."

"I've had a little practice at this," he said.

She nodded and then scanned the bracelet over the plate where it glowed red. And then it turned green and there was the sound of a lock clicking as the gate unlatched. The challenge was for them to both squeeze through the small gate. They embraced and then scooted through as one. No problem.

"Now what?" she whispered.

"Let's get the box and get out of here."

"Don't you want to look around? Maybe try to get back in the room where Buck was found?"

"Actually, going inside the house adds an extra layer to this," he said.

"I want to see what's in the drawer," she whispered. She felt his forearm tense, and she realized he was reaching for his weapon. Fear spiked inside of her, and she could feel her pulse thumping in her throat. "What is it?"

"I heard someone," Hank said. "Follow me and stay close."

It was then she heard it too. Precise, almost angry footsteps across a manicured gravel pathway.

Hank grabbed her and hurried her toward the shadows, finally picking her up so they didn't make too much noise. They followed the edge of the fence at the back of the house, and the smell of chlorine from the pool grew stronger. She could see the glint of the water in the moonlight, but the house was completely dark.

Her breaths were coming in hard pants when they stopped near the gazebo. "Who is it?"

"How would I know?" he said.

Lights began to turn on, section by section. They were still safe, but if they kept turning on lights they'd eventually be seen.

"It's them," Agatha hissed. "Ritzo and Kraken."

"I can only imagine what they're up to alone in the dark," Hank whispered. "I wouldn't be surprised if they broke into Heather's house while she's in lockup so they could pilfer and then plant a few things around the crime scene."

The reality of this entire farce was becoming too real and too much to deal with. At what point would the cavalry arrive? Good is supposed to conquer evil. How could these two detectives exercise so much power without accountability?

"I really hate them," she said.

Hank's grip tightened on her arm, but it was too late. They'd heard something and turned to look in their direction.

"What do we do?" she asked.

"We just go further into the field."

"The security lights will expose us," she said.

They were crouched down behind the gazebo, and her thighs were beginning to burn. They could see over the railing and the light was at the detective's backs. They were still a good distance away, but it wouldn't be long before they were right on top of them.

"We need to hide," she said.

"Where? We can't stay here. They're heading this way."

"The hot tub."

"You want to hold your breath in a hot tub?" Hank asked.

Ritzo was a few steps ahead of Kraken. He held a flashlight. The powerful beam scanned back and forth across the open area. It wouldn't be long until they wouldn't be able to run or hide without getting exposed. She had to do something.

"If I remember right, the hot tub isn't filled to the brim."

"Here's to hoping your memory is right and their ears are dull," Hank said.

Hank grabbed her hand and they moved toward the Olympic sized pool with the ridiculous fountain of the mermaids in the middle. Unfortunately, the fountain wasn't on. There was a stone wall that led down into a lagoon style hot tub.

Agatha could hear the two men talking. Their voices were unsure and angry. She could tell that they were there just like she and Hank—without permission. The difference was what each duo was willing to do to avoid detection.

"Stay low, and on this cement," Hank said softly. "They'll see footprints in the grass."

Agatha was amazed that Hank's mind was processing information so fast, and under such duress. She was doing good not to fall over in a dead faint.

"They're moving in," she said. "What are we going to do?"

"Go," he said. "Now."

The urgency was unmistakable. They ran in the dark toward the hot tub, and Agatha rolled into the lagoon-style hot tub. She saw Hank take his gun out and set it within arm's reach before he did the same.

The water was warm, and they moved to the inside edge and waited, breaths as quiet as they could manage. Her eyes had adjusted to the dark, but it was even darker inside the hot tub with the lush foliage surrounding them. She barely heard the sound of him releasing his magazine from his pistol, and he took a couple of bullets out before he put the magazine back in.

Agatha stared in wide-eyed confusion as he took the bullets in his hand and threw them as far as he could in the opposite direction.

"Over there," she heard one of the detectives say. And then she breathed out a sigh of relief and settled in to wait for their chance to escape.

Chapter Fourteen

HANK WANTED to stay in bed. The night before definitely wasn't on his top ten list of great date nights. They'd been stuck in that hot tub for more than an hour before they'd been able to escape and make their way back to the car.

Hank rolled out of bed and went into the kitchen so he could enjoy his breakfast of a banana and an Ensure. He was just as much a creature of habit as Agatha was.

Coil had text messaged him earlier to say he was stopping by, and Hank had given him an abbreviated rundown of what they'd learned so far. He'd told Coil he'd be out back having breakfast. He liked sitting at the little table on his patio, watching the birds and looking at his roses. It was peaceful. And retired people were supposed to do stuff like that instead of hiding from the cops in a hot tub.

Hank had been thinking about Buck's will. Candy, Ritzo, and Kraken had to be in on it together. It made perfect sense. Candy somehow found out about the will, which means she'd know that if Heather went to prison, she could contest it and become Buck's beneficiary since she was his legal wife at time of death. All Candy had to do was promise Ritzo and Kraken a cut of the money, and then their investigation would turn toward Heather and stay there.

"It's me," Coil called out and opened the back gate.

"Come on back," Hank said. "There's fresh coffee inside."

Coil nodded and went into the kitchen and then came back a couple of minutes later with a mug of coffee. He wore his habitual uniform of jeans and a western-style shirt, this one in tan, and his badge and gun were at his waist.

"Heard you got a little wet last night," Coil said as he folded his long, wiry body into the chair next to Hank.

"It was an interesting night," Hank said. "I'd prefer not to have another one like it. Retired people aren't supposed to do stuff like that."

"Technically, no one is supposed to do stuff like that. It's against the law."

Hank smiled and acknowledged him with his bottle of Ensure. "I was hoping you'd be able to help us out with the next step in this mess. I'm guessing the police chief and the mayor are still staying out of reach?"

"Yep," Coil said. "They're not going to touch this until they see which way the wind is blowing. "I agree with you that it looks like Candy is playing for the money shot and those two guerillas are helping her out."

"What do we do next?"

"Can you talk to Candy?"

"Doubtful," Hank said.

"Then run the end around. There are other ex-wives who were at that party and talked to Buck."

"You're right," Hank said. "One of them had to see him dead on the edge of the bed and rolled him over. Even if they thought he was sleeping. The body was definitely moved post-mortem.

"Aren't they all nurses?" Coil reminded him.

Hank dropped his head. He knew Reggie was right. There was no medical misunderstanding involved in Buck's death. Someone either killed him or knew he'd died and was purposefully trying to turn it against Heather.

Hank's phone rang. It was Agatha.

"Morning, Aggie," he said, his smile automatic in anticipation of hearing her voice.

"Hank, I need you right now," Agatha said.

"No good mornings?" he asked.

"Get over her now," she said, and hung up.

Hank felt a sense of panic. What if she was in danger? Maybe Ritzo and Kraken discovered it was her last night.

"Come on, Coil. Something's up. She might be in trouble. Hank sprinted through his home to throw on a shirt and shoes, and he grabbed his gun. Coil was already on his way to Agatha's when Hank ran out the front door and down the street.

Hank and Coil rushed toward Agatha's front porch, and Hank took the three steps in a single leap. Agatha opened the door, a huge smile on her face. Hank hesitated for a moment. It was too odd, and maybe she was acting under duress.

"Are you okay?" Hank asked, trying to see any signs of strain on her face or body language.

"I'm great," she said. "Now get in here." She reached out and grabbed him by the arm and pulled him inside.

"Umm," Coil said. "This seems like a personal matter. I guess I'll leave."

"You get in here too," she said, and she pulled him in just like she'd done Hank.

She headed toward the war room, and both men followed, completely puzzled.

"I couldn't sleep after my night of hot tubbing," she said. "So, I put the pics back on the wall. The sandal bothered you, but you weren't sure why."

"You found something?" Hank asked.

"I wondered why the sandal wasn't all the way beneath the bed if it got kicked hard enough for it to get flipped upside down and sideways. I researched the bed Buck was found dead on. Other than being ridiculously expensive, it isn't hollow underneath."

"There's no under bed access?" Coil asked.

"Correct," she said, pointing at him like a good student.

"And?" Hank asked.

"When the sandal was kicked, it could only go so far. So, I zoomed in on this particular area of the sandal. Ever stub a toe?"

"Sure," Hank said.

"So did whoever kicked that sandal," Agatha said. "But I bet neither of you stubbed a toe after a fresh pedicure."

She brought an image into focus on the wall screen. It was the very edge of the sandal's sole. There were carpet fibers and flakes of orange stuck onto the rubber sole.

"Orange?" Coil asked, "How in the world are we going to match that to someone at the party? We don't have crime lab access for those samples."

Agatha clucked her tongue as she waited for Hank's reply. Hank felt his blood begin to pump as his mind raced back over every detail from Saturday night at Buck's party. She was prompting him to recall a very specific detail. He enjoyed the cat and mouse because he knew she'd already figured it out.

"Okay, I'll take a stab," Hank walked toward the picture. "It was a fourth of July celebration, and in Texas at that. I couldn't imagine a more patriotic gathering, nor can I fathom anyone crazy enough to not arrive decked out in good old American red, white and blue."

"Getting warmer," Agatha said.

"Except not everyone at the party was feeling patriotic," he said. "Someone was wearing Buck's favorite color instead. Just in case."

"Bingo," Agatha said.

"I'll admit," Hank said. "I have no idea if her toenails were painted orange."

"Let a woman assure you," Agatha said. "You'd better believe her toenails matched. Matching is everything."

"Looks like we know where we're heading next," Hank said. "I'll be back to pick you up once I change clothes."

"Are you sure?" she asked. "I think your weapon looks kind of cute with your pajama bottoms."

Chapter Fifteen

THERESA HAZARD LIVED IN FORT WORTH, AND HER HOME was relatively tame compared to what her settlement from Buck could've afforded. It was nestled in a gated-community and on a cul-de-sac street, though the gate didn't do much good at keeping them out since it was wide open. Her house was a two-story Greek revival with large white columns across the front, and she had a meticulously manicured front lawn.

Hank thought it was best to show up unannounced. Agatha, on the other hand, didn't think a woman would appreciate a surprise visit without the chance to get herself fixed up. They'd soon see who was right.

Hank pulled into a circular driveway and parked right in front of the front doors. There was a giant fountain with a Greek statue in the center.

Hank rang the bell, and they only waited a few moments before it opened.

"Detective," Theresa said, her smile saying she remembered him very well.

He felt the color rise in his cheeks as Agatha stared him

down. It didn't help that Theresa was wearing nothing more than a couple of scraps of black cloth for a bathing suit. There was nothing left to the imagination.

"Good to see you again, Theresa," he said. "This is my partner, Agatha Harley."

"Partner?" Theresa asked, raising her brows and looking Agatha over like she was day old meatloaf. "Where's the sexy cowboy?"

"With his wife and seven kids," Agatha said blandly.

"Wow," she said, eyes wide with surprise. "Seven children. There's something very attractive about a man who's that virile.

"Do you mind if we speak with you for a few minutes?" Hank asked her. "I just want to follow up after we spoke the other night."

"I'm about to go layout," she said. "I'm on a tight schedule today, and this is my only time to relax by myself."

Hank took a step forward because it looked like she wanted to shut the door in their faces. A weariness had come into her eyes the minute he'd asked if they could talk. He took a quick glance down at her toenails. He recognized the color.

"What happened to your toenail?" he asked.

"I stubbed it out by the pool this morning," she said. "It's no big deal."

"You know, Theresa," Hank said. "I don't think you meant to do it." If he hadn't been watching her so closely, he never would've seen the slight widening of her eyes and the subtle hitch in her breath.

"I don't know what you're talking about," she said.

"Do you really want to play this game?" Hank asked.

Theresa blew out a breath a dropped her head against the door. She spoke soft and low. "How'd you know?"

"We've been investigating this since Saturday night," Hank said. "The evidence, and let's just say other people at the party, led us to you."

"Well, shoot," she said. "Y'all might as well come in. I need a drink."

"It's ten o'clock in the morning," Agatha said, following her inside.

"It's five o'clock somewhere," Theresa called out over her shoulder.

Hank turned his phone recorder on while Theresa's back was turned, and he shut the front door behind them.

"Y'all want anything?" she asked. "Bloody Mary? Screwdriver? Mimosa?"

"We're fine," Hank said.

The kitchen was meant for entertaining, and Theresa moved to the Sub-Zero refrigerator and pulled out a glass pitcher of orange juice. She grabbed a bottle of vodka from the freezer and then poured a generous helping into a large glass and gave it a splash of orange juice for color.

"Holy cow," Agatha whispered.

The entire back of the house was floor to ceiling windows that looked out over a beautiful pool and patio area. Theresa balanced her drink in one hand and then pushed the sliding glass door all the way into the wall so the inside and outside flowed seamlessly.

"Come on back," she said. "The sun is just right this time of the morning."

Hank raised his brows and then gestured for Agatha to go ahead of him.

"She's a fruit loop," Agatha whispered as she passed by.

But Hank didn't think so. He'd gotten the impression the other night that she was more intelligent than she liked to let on. She wasn't a ditzy airhead.

Theresa took a long sip of her drink and then set it on a glass table next to a lounge chair. And then she laid a towel on her padded beach chair, and without any modesty at all, she took off her bathing suit top and draped it over the back of the chair before laying face down.

"Ahh," Hank said, trying to figure out where he was supposed to look.

"Fruit loop," Agatha mouthed, circling her finger around her temple.

"Y'all have a seat," she said. "Might as well make yourselves comfortable."

"Tell us what happened Ms. Hazard," Hank said.

She was face down in the towel, but Hank could mostly make out what she was saying. "I was so excited when I got the invitation to the party. When we were married, the Fourth of July bash was my favorite time of the year, and I haven't been since we got divorced.

"I got the invite and I immediately picked up the phone and called him because, well, I thought it might have been a mistake with the invitations. But he was in a great mood and assured me that it was no mistake, and that he couldn't wait to see me. Just like with Lorraine, he brought up the past, those happy, sappy memories that make you smile. And when we hung up the phone, I just knew there was still something between us, and that whatever big news he wanted to tell me at the party had to do with our future.

"Did it?" Agatha asked.

"Nope," she said. "Just the opposite." She turned her head and looked straight at them, and there was no mistaking the anger in her eyes. He gave me a hug and a kiss on the cheek and told me I would always hold a special place in his heart, but he was holding onto the past and it was time to let go.

"I asked him flat out what he was talking about, and he poured himself a Scotch and then said he wanted to make his marriage with Candy work. That he was getting too old to do the marriage-go-round anymore, and he enjoyed her company well enough. He said for them to have a fresh start it meant letting go of his past and cutting the rest of us off from our monthly stipend. He blathered on about how he hoped we'd invested our money wisely, but I didn't really hear anything but the blood rushing in my ears after that.

"Of course, I haven't been investing," she whined. "Buck's monthly support check was my investment. I'm not going back to nursing. I can tell you that. I just don't know what I'm supposed to do." She blinked rapidly as her eyes tried to fill with tears, but Hank thought she needed to go back to acting school to make it believable.

"Did you see him often?" Hank asked.

"We saw each other at social events from time to time," she said. "And I've dated one or two of his associates. Can you rub lotion on my back?" Theresa asked, holding a brown bottle out to Hank.

"No, I don't think so," Hank said.

"I'll do it," Agatha said with a gleam in her eyes, and then she made a motion for him to wrap it up.

Theresa looked at Agatha warily, but she handed over the bottle. Agatha shook the bottle with a little too much enthusiasm and squirted a cold stream of white right down the middle of Theresa's back. She screeched and reared up, but Agatha put the flat of her hand against Theresa's back and pushed her back down since she was flashing everyone. Then she rubbed the lotion in with all the tenderness of Nurse Ratched.

Hank coughed to cover his laugh.

"Look," Theresa said. "I was angry. But I didn't kill

him. I started yelling and telling him the girls and I wouldn't stand for it. He'd made us a promise and by the time we were done with him we'd own everything. I didn't really notice how bad his color got because I was just so mad, but he grabbed for his chest.

"A heart attack," Agatha whispered.

"Yep," she said. "And at the moment I felt like the Lord was on my side. He reached for the nitroglycerin tablets in his nightstand, but it was too late. I've seen massive heart attacks before and there was nothing a whole team of medical people could've done for him. He was dead in less than a minute.

"You're a nurse," Hank said. "Why would you just stand there and watch him die, and not try to help him?"

"I used to be a nurse," she corrected. "And why in the world would I look a gift horse in the mouth when God made him have a heart attack? That seems ungrateful."

"It seems negligent and cruel to me," Agatha said, wiping her hands on the towel and standing up. "But what do I know?"

"And now Buck is dead, and you'll lose the monthly stipend anyway," Hank said.

"Oh, no," she said. "He always told us our stipend would continue even after he was long gone. Really, this was a win-win for everyone."

"Except Buck," Agatha said. "Because he's *dead*."

Theresa shrugged. "He died of natural causes. No crime in that."

"What did you do after he died?"

Theresa rolled over so she was face up, and Hank quickly looked up at the ceiling(sky?). He heard Agatha say, "I'm not rubbing lotion on those," and he coughed again to cover his snicker.

"I went and told Candy," Theresa said. "She's his wife,

after all, and I figure she could deal with the cleanup. But she told me she wasn't going to let Buck ruin the party for her whether he was dead or alive, and she told me if I breathed a word to anyone, she'd make sure that I took the blame. She told me she had a contingency plan in the case Buck died and to leave well enough alone. So, I got another margarita and rejoined the party."

"What kind of contingency plan?" Hank asked.

"Something about how Heather was still the beneficiary in Buck's will, and there was only one way to make sure she never saw a red hot cent. We all knew Heather was always his favorite, but I figured she was getting a stipend like the rest of us. I didn't realize she'd be getting the whole enchilada when Buck finally keeled over."

Theresa chewed on her lip for a moment and then looked at them. "Do you think I'm going to get in trouble? I didn't kill him. But I saw what those detectives did to Heather, and I am not going to jail. I'm accustomed to a certain way of living, and jail doesn't live up to that standard."

"I think the more you help us, the more you'll help yourself," Hank said in a very official voice.

"What more can I do?"

"Candy wants to get control of everything," Agatha said. "She thinks with Buck dead and Heather going to prison for murder, she'll just step in and contest the will so she will be the one getting the inheritance."

Theresa snorted. "Sounds just like her. It's not like she wasn't obvious about going after Buck and his money. Heck, I knew her back before all the plastic surgery and dye job. She made herself look like Buck's type and then swooped in for the kill. It isn't right."

"Do you think you could call Candy and tell her that you changed your mind about staying quiet because you're afraid the cops will find out the truth?" Agatha asked. "Tell her you're nervous because of how they've falsely accused Heather. We'd like to record the entire conversation."

Hank texted coil. If Theresa could get Candy to spill the beans, then law enforcement would have to get involved. The Texas Rangers would be the best agency to turn to, because they didn't have a dog in the fight. With Ritzo and Kraken and the corruption that surrounded them, an outside agency was the only way to keep things by the book.

"I'll do it," Theresa said. "That baboon-faced booty call isn't getting Buck's money."

It didn't take long for Coil to text back saying the Rangers were a go, and he gave Agatha a thumbs up.

"Is there a robe I could get you so you can make the call?" Hank asked.

"It's too hot for a robe," she said. "I've got a sarong hanging over that chair."

Agatha handed her the sarong, and Theresa got up and wrapped it around her waist, not bothering to cover her bare chest at all.

Hank rolled his eyes, and Agatha whacked herself in the forehead with the palm of her hand. And they followed Theresa back inside. She led them into a room with a lot of animal print used in the decorating, and bold slashes of red to add color. But it mostly looked like a safari that had ended badly for all the animals.

"Just give me a second to get connected to Bluetooth," Hank said, "And you can make the call.

Hank handed her a set of Bluetooth headphones and they tested them out before Hank gave Theresa the go-ahead to make the call.

"Remember what we talked about and stick to it,"

Agatha reminded her. "Otherwise Candy will end up with all Buck's money, and you might end up in jail."

Theresa nodded, her blue eyes big and round.

"Why are you calling this number?" Candy said by way of answering.

Candy's tone immediately had Theresa's back going up, and her nervousness disappeared. "To sell you cellulite remover. I saw you in your bathing suit the other night."

Candy gasped. "Why you…"

"Oh, put a cork in it, Candy. You never could take a joke," Theresa said.

Maybe Hank hadn't given her enough credit for her acting skills. She was doing beautifully.

"I'm actually calling about something serious," Theresa said. "I've been thinking a lot about Buck's death, and what you told me to do, but I just can't do it anymore." Her voice went low and somber. "I feel terrible."

"Is this some kind of sick joke?" Candy asked. "Because I will kill you with my own two hands."

"Get a grip, Candy," she said. "This isn't a joke anymore. Your husband is dead."

"Yeah," she said. "*My* husband. But guess who will walk away with all his money if you don't keep your fat trap shut? You think I'm going to let you talk? Buck died of a heart attack," Candy said. "So what? But that little floozie Heather could've made him have one just as easily as you did. You're all bleeding my money from him, so I don't care if you all die or go to jail."

"You can threaten me all you want, but you're just as guilty. I told you he was dead, and you're the one who came in and moved the body. You're the one who lied to the police about Heather. So if I go to jail, you'd better believe you're coming with me."

LILIANA HART & LOUIS SCOTT

"How much do you want?" Candy said, all seriousness now. "Name your price. All I'm asking you to do is to stay drunk until tomorrow morning when they can formally charge her for murder. It'll be national news. And as soon as Buck's will is settled, I'll pay you in cash. I already owe Ritzo and Kraken, though I had to pay them up front."

"Yeah, I don't really work on a lay-a-way plan either," Theresa said, playing along.

"Give me two hours to come up with the cash," Candy said. "I'll call you back and we'll settle this. Just keep your mouth shut."

Candy hung up, and Theresa handed the headphones back to Hank. "Will that help?" she asked.

"Absolutely," Hank said. "We appreciate it."

Agatha snapped a quick photograph of Theresa's chipped toenail.

"What are you doing?" Theresa asked

"Just in case Candy's offer is too tempting to pass up," Agatha said. "Don't let us down, Theresa."

Chapter Sixteen

THE ONLY PLACE OPEN IN RUSTY GUN ON THE MONDAY following a Fourth of July holiday was the Taco and Waffle. It was about ten o'clock at night and he and Agatha had already had a margarita and three bowls of chips and salsa while they waited on Coil. Actually, Agatha had eaten all the salsa. Hank had to go easy on the spicy stuff. He liked it, but at fifty-four, it didn't like him too much.

Coil finally came through the door and immediately removed his cowboy hat as he said hello to the hostess.

"Hey, Coil," Hank said as Coil slipped into the booth with them. "Long day, huh?"

Coil placed his Stetson on the hook outside the booth. His eyes were bloodshot, and there were dark purple smudges under his eyes.

"The two of you are a pain in the behind," Coil said. "I should've known you wouldn't let it rest after I talked to you this morning."

"It's the least we could do for Heather," Hank said.

"Oh, so you're a fan of Heather's now?" Coil teased.

"No, I'm a fan of justice. I'm also a fan of making Kraken and Ritzo's lives miserable. So, I got to kill two birds with one stone."

"What's going to happen to them?" Agatha asked, eating more chips and sipping from her schooner of strawberry margarita.

"Since you got Candy to confess that she'd paid off Kraken and Ritzo, the Texas Rangers were able to take over. I can tell you you're going to owe Will and Whitehorse big. The medical examiner hadn't gotten around to doing the autopsy on Buck since, no doubt, Kraken and Ritzo had convinced him to wait until they were able to make an arrest. Will and Whitehorse had Sweet pick up the body, and he conducted the autopsy this afternoon. COD is officially a myocardial infarction."

"Just like Theresa told us," Hank said. "Heart attack. So, what's next?"

Coil reached across the table and grabbed Hank's drink glass. It was frosted over and rimmed with salt. He sipped and set it back down.

"Thought you didn't drink?" Hank asked.

"I don't," Coil said, "I sipped."

That small gesture bothered Hank, but he kept his mouth shut. For now.

"I wasn't there," Coil said, "But Will Ellis said Candy sang like a bird. She cleared Heather, and Theresa will likely get a slap on the wrist for being stupid, but she'll probably just pay a fine and do community service. But Candy hammered nails into the careers of your all-time favorite detectives."

"Will they be arrested?" Agatha asked.

"Tomorrow," Coil said. "The Rangers are working with the state's attorney general on preparing arrest warrants, for everything from falsifying official documents to kidnapping and wrongful imprisonment."

"What about Heather?" Hank asked.

"They thought it was best to wait until Ritzo and Kraken were removed from the scene before releasing her. It's for her own safety, and also as to not tip off either detective."

"That's hardly fair," Agatha said, smacking her hand on the table. "She's got to spend a whole other night in that rat hole."

"Sorry, Agatha, but her safety and everyone else's come before her convenience," Coil said. "They'd know the gig was up if she got sprung free. They'd go on a rampage to quiet any potential witnesses," Coil explained. "Especially if they felt they were being closed in on. They're armed and dangerous. Plus, it looks like Heather is going to fall into another massive payday once she settles a lawsuit with the city of Dallas for the way this was handled."

"Not like she's going to need the money," Hank said. "She's entitled to millions from Buck's estate."

"How'd she do it?" Coil said with a whistle.

"It's not like she planned for it to happen." Agatha snapped. "She gives her whole heart to her relationships, but Heather's got lots of hurt in her life that no marriage will ever heal."

"What about Karl?" Hank asked.

"Poor kid's been worried sick about her," Coil said. "I told him to steer clear, and he has, but it doesn't mean he hasn't been afraid of losing her."

"I'll be there to pick her up, and treat her to a girl's day," Agatha said. "She's going to need to decompress.

"Keep it low key," Coil warned. "Not everyone is going to believe she was innocent, nor will people be happy that two long-time and very productive police detectives were arrested. Like it or not, they were respected by the city, as well as feared."

Agatha clicked her tongue and pointed a finger gun at Coil. "You got it, sheriff."

"How many margaritas have you had?" Coil asked.

"She's had about three sips of that one," Hank said, grinning, but you know she's a lightweight."

"By the way, Agatha," Coil said. "The Rangers recovered the electronic box that had the date and time stamp of all the party guests. It seems like you went to the party twice, and one of those times was last night when there was no one at home. I think they have some questions for you."

Agatha just grinned sloppily and rested her head against Hank's shoulder. "We were like Remington Steele," she told Coil, and then fell asleep against Hank.

"She's put in a lot of hours," Hank said, laughing.

"I'd be worn out too if Heather was my friend," Coil said. "Y'all head home and get some sleep. I'm going to do the same. Coil slipped a twenty-dollar bill on the table.

"No need Reggie," Hank said. "I got it."

"No," Coil said. "Y'all didn't give up on her when everyone else did. Heather needed friends and y'all were there. I hope if I ever need that effort that you'd fight for me that hard."

"You know I would," Hank said, grabbing Coil's wrist. "Everything okay?"

"Sure, why you ask?"

Now that Hank got a closer look at him, he realized he didn't look good at all. "You surprised me when you took that drink."

"It was just a sip," Coil said.

"It's never just a sip, and you know that," Hank said. "So, I'm going to ask you again, are you okay?"

Coil sighed and dropped back into the booth. "I'm just not sure how this is going to unfold."

"You mean with Ritzo and Kraken going down tomorrow?"

Coil nodded.

"You thinking something might come back on you?" Hank asked. "From the old days?"

"I sure as heck hope not," Coil said.

"You know I'm always here to fight for you," Hank said. "Whatever it takes."

"Brothers," Coil said.

"Brothers," Hank agreed.

Epilogue

HEATHER HADN'T SAID a word the entire drive back from Dallas. She looked shell shocked, and rightfully so. She was still dressed in the electric blue outfit from Saturday night, and it was obvious they'd not allowed her to shower or practice any hygiene. Agatha would never say it aloud, but Heather needed a root touch up something fierce. Confinement wasn't good to her. Agatha was afraid Heather had some form of PTSD by the way she was acting.

They made a quick stop at Heather's house so she could shower and change. Agatha took Hank's advice and kept Heather protected and isolated in Rusty Gun. It was time to get pampered, and they were heading to the only place the town had to offer.

Glamour Shots Studio and Nail Salon was downtown, and the AC was working overtime between the heat and all the chemicals floating around inside.

Agatha was dressed in her usual yoga pants and an olive drab, sleeveless sports top, and her pants were rolled up to her knees as her feet soaked in a whirling bath.

"Girl," Heather said, sipping on a glass of boxed wine the owner had poured her as soon as they came in. "I've got no idea what I'm going to do about Buck's funeral. It says in the will that he wants me to send him off in style, and I'm the only one he trusts to do it just how he'd like it. That's a lot of pressure."

Heather's hair was wrapped in tin-foil and her head was stuck under a dryer.

"Why?" Agatha asked. "Funeral homes do this every day. Just hire a good one, get a band and a caterer and you've got yourself a funeral."

"It has to be spectacular," she said. "Everyone is going to be staring at me. They hate me."

"When have you ever cared about that?" Agatha asked.

A tear slipped down Heather's cheek. "Never," she said, barely audible over the hair dryer. "It's not really about me. I just don't want to be a distraction. He deserves to be honored for the generous man he was."

"I can understand that, and it's very sweet that you've considered Buck's wishes first." Agatha said. "I'm sure you'll do exactly what he wants."

"What he'd want is for all the women to show up in bikinis, and for the strippers he liked to watch every week do a headliner show. He'd want streamers and booze and a heck of a party. He'd want it to last a whole week, just like John McCain, with all the pomp and circumstance he felt he deserved."

"Well..." Agatha said. Because she couldn't think of anything else other than she really hoped Heather didn't asked her to be her plus one for the funeral.

Dot Williams owned the shop, but she'd never done hair a day in her life, so she hired two stylists to take care of hair and nails, and she dealt with the glamour shot side of things. Dot kept watching their conversation like a tennis match, but she couldn't hear all the gossip because she was trying to help three high school seniors decide which backdrop would look the least hideous for their graduation pics.

"Whatever you do," Agatha said, "I'm sure it'll be amazing."

"I love you so much, Agatha," Heather said, tearing up. "You're my best friend in the whole world, and if I hadn't had you during all this, I just don't know what I would've done."

Dot harrumphed. "If you'd been with your man in Rusty Gun instead of playing the merry widow over and over again just so you can take their money, maybe you wouldn't end up in these situations."

Heather gasped and would've come up out of the chair if her head hadn't been stuck in the dryer.

"How about you mind your own business," Agatha said.

"I don't have to watch anything," she said. "This is my shop, and I'm tired of hearing about your hoity-toity problems. Maybe a salon in the city would be more your style."

"Oh, it is," Heather said. "But I like to patronize local businesses so they have a fighting chance. I'm happy to stop that though and tell all my friends to do the same."

Agatha's eyes widened and she took her feet out of the water just in case she had to break up a fight.

"Ooh, I'm so scared," Dot said. "Everybody knows you don't have any friends. No one's going to listen to you. How about you rich girls learn how to work for a living instead of depending on men to suck dry."

"Umm…" Agatha said. "I work hard, and I've earned every penny I've ever made. Your jealousy is showing Dot. And green isn't a pretty color on you."

Dot scowled at her. "Yeah, writing words on a page is really hard. Give me a break. And this one," she said, pointing at Heather, "Apparently works her way through the town on her back. I didn't know prostitution was legal in Rusty Gun. Maybe I need to bring it up at the council meeting."

"Are you on drugs, Dot?" Agatha asked. "Or maybe you need to be."

"I went out to walk my dog the other night and this one and Deputy Karl were going at it behind the water plant. What? The pay by the hour motel wasn't good enough for you? I was stuck there until they finished."

"Or you could've turned around and walked away, pervert," Heather said. "Once again, mind your own business you sicko."

"If Sheriff Coil was doing his job, maybe this type of public fornication would end," she said. "If he's going to let his deputies whore around with the city trash, then the whole town is doomed."

Heather and Agatha both gasped at that, and Agatha jumped up and took a step between Heather and Dot. The foil on Heather's head was all but shooting with electricity.

"Let's get out of here, Heather," Agatha said. "She clearly doesn't need the business, and she'll never get mine again."

"Oh, I don't know," Heather said a little too sweetly. "Wouldn't it be nice to go around and tell everyone who did my hair today? You'd like that, wouldn't you, Dot? To service the town trash?" Heather's words were clipped and furious, but there was a rage inside them that scared Agatha to death, and Dot must've seen it too.

Heather pulled the foils out of her hair one by one and dropped them on the ground.

"You don't scare me," Dot said. "And unlike everyone else, you can't buy me. Things will be very different with a new sheriff in town."

"A new sheriff?" Agatha asked. "Yeah, right."

"Oddie (Odie?) McElroy is gonna set this county straight. He's from Belton, and he's more qualified to be Sheriff of this place. Coil belongs in jail with those two dirty cops that just got arrested." Dot's smile was pure evil. "I know things you could only hope to know. Change in Rusty Gun is coming."

Dot's words caused an ominous feeling to prickle the hairs on Agatha's arms, but she and Heather grabbed their purses, put on their shoes, and opened the door.

"I think the chemicals have gone to your brain, Dot Williams," Agatha said. "You're nothing but trouble. But I can tell you, whatever you've got cooked up behind that evil smile, will get you nothing but trouble. If you try to cause trouble for us or Sheriff Coil, he'll bury you. And no wannabe from Belton is going to swoop in and save you."

With that, Agatha slammed the door behind her and walked out into the harsh summer sun.

"I need to find Hank," Agatha said.

"And I need to get this bleach out of my hair before it all falls out. Thanks for busting me out of prison, but I'm tired now and am going home. Take it from someone who has experienced jail. Don't do anything stupid where Dot is concerned."

"I'll be fine," Agatha said. Heather's hair was stiff and white and stuck up in tufts from where she'd pulled out the foil. She looked a sight. "But I wouldn't be heartbroken if her business burned to the ground."

Heather shot her a grin and then got in the passenger seat of Agatha's Jeep. "You're a good friend. Now get me to a sink as fast as you can."

Sneak Peek: Tequila Mockingbird

Download Now - Tequila Mockingbird

Tuesday

The first hints of fall blew in with a bite, the leaves shivering on the trees and the clouds fighting to hide the sun. But for Agatha Harley, October brought melancholy and other emotions she wasn't entirely comfortable dealing with. Her parents had been married in October some sixty years before. And they died in October a decade ago.

She'd missed her jog that morning, and instead, lingered under the covers until the scent of coffee she'd timed to brew the night before had lured her into the kitchen. She'd slept in gray sweats and thick fuzzy socks in orange and white stripes, and she'd shuffled out onto the front porch to drink her coffee and try to get her thoughts under control.

Hank had messaged her asking if she'd wanted company. He'd remembered. And despite having that tough guy exterior and an intimidation factor that could scare people away at twenty paces, he had a sweet heart.

But she hadn't wanted company. Her mood called for solitude.

The caffeine began to clear the fog from her mind, and she tried to think of business instead of her parents. She owed her literary agent an answer on the offer she'd gotten for a movie option for her next book, which wasn't even finished yet. At one point in her life, this part of her career would have been exciting, but her heart just wasn't in it.

The sun chose that moment to peek around the clouds, and Agatha put her hand up to block it from her eyes. She was thinking of Hank, wondering if he was sitting on his back porch like he liked to do in the mornings, and wondered if she shouldn't pay him a visit. Or it would be even better if he completely ignored her request to be alone and showed up at her place.

"Good morning."

Agatha startled and looked around the tall hedges at the corner of the house to where the voice had come from. White dots danced in front of her eyes from the sun's brightness, so she couldn't make out who it was.

"Hank?" she asked.

"Oh, no dear," a voice said with a tinkling laugh. "It's me. Edna Merth from next door."

Edna Merth was a fixture in Rusty Gun. There was no telling how old she was, but she was probably only a generation or two removed from the original settlers. She'd lived in the little blue and white Craftsman home since before her parents had married.

"You okay, honey?" Edna asked, moving unsteadily over the uneven ground until she stood in front of Agatha.

She was short—maybe five feet tall—and almost as round as she was tall. Her hair was thick and white, and she wore it in a bun on top of her head. Agatha had never seen her without an apron on. Today's was lemon yellow with bright red cherries on it.

"I'm okay, Ms. Edna," Agatha lied. "I'm just enjoying the weather." And the solitude, she added silently.

"Shouldn't you be out for your morning run?" Edna asked, resting her hands on her round belly. "I do enjoy watching you whiz by in the mornings. Your outfits are always so colorful. We couldn't wear things like that in my day. Especially not in Rusty Gun. Always were a bunch of nosy hypocrites in this town."

Agatha raised her brows at that. In her lifetime, she'd maybe had a handful of conversations with Edna Merth, and nothing deeper than the surface of a casual hello or how's the weather. Edna had always been very active in the community, but progressing Alzheimer's over the past decade had left her withdrawn and secluded.

"I'll try to get a run in tonight," Agatha said. "I just wasn't feeling up to it this morning.

Edna clicked her tongue and nodded solemnly. She had a full-time nurse who stayed with her, and Agatha peeped around Edna's girth to see if anyone else had followed Edna into the yard. But it was just Edna. All by herself.

"Ms. Edna, does Darleen know you're outside?"

"I'm supposed to be napping," she said with considerable mischief in her eyes. "I always take a nap after breakfast and my meds, but I just pretended this morning. Sometimes I do that. Darleen likes to nap after breakfast too while she's watching Price is Right."

Agatha's lips twitched, but she knew it wasn't a laughing matter. Edna seemed just fine right now, but that wasn't always the case.

"You know Darleen will be worried half to death if she wakes up and sees you gone," Agatha said.

Did you know Jim Brown killed his wife and buried her?" Edna said, plucking at the little red berries that grew on the bushes next to the house.

"Ahh," Agatha said, looking again for Darleen to appear. "Jim Brown from the hardware store?"

Edna looked around to see if anyone was watching, and then lowered her voice to a whisper. "Oh, yes. He walks his dog every night and goes to visit his her. Carol was a nice woman. Kind of quiet, but very polite any time I went to the hardware store. He must feel a lot of guilt, I think."

"I thought that was just a rumor," Agatha said.

Edna had started humming to herself, and she was picking the little red berries and putting them in her apron pocket.

"I remember their wedding," she said.

"Jim and Carol's?" Agatha asked.

Edna's face went completely blank with confusion. "Who are Jim and Carol?" she asked. "Your parents, dear. They had a lovely wedding."

Agatha's mouth went dry. She didn't know how they'd gone from talking about Jim Brown killing his wife to her parent's wedding, but there they were. And how odd for Edna to touch on something that had been so heavy on her heart all morning.

They were so young and in love," Edna added with a soft sigh. "I'm sorry for your loss. They were wonderful people."

She felt the tears welling in her eyes, so she buried her face in the oversized coffee cup she held and inhaled the warmth.

"I know you miss them," Edna continued. "Emory and Elaine were wonderful to have as friends and neighbors, even though Tom and I were old enough to be their parents. I can imagine they were even better to have as parents."

Agatha flinched at the touch of gentle fingers on her shoulder.

"They were," Agatha said, her voice catching. She was an introvert—a solitary person by choice—but it was rare she felt lonely as she did today.

"I didn't mean to intrude," Edna said. "But I knew today was the anniversary of their terrible accident, and I wanted to tell you how special they were."

"I hadn't even realized it was today," she said. "And yes, they were very special. I appreciate you coming over to tell me. It means a lot. I don't know why it's hitting me so hard this year."

"I lost my Thomas over twenty years ago, and I still have bad days. There are days I miss him so much I can still smell his scent in the house, or the way the mattress dipped when he got into bed. Grief is a strange and terrible thing. But it's important to grieve. It's healthy."

Agatha scooted over on the porch step so Edna could wedge in next to her.

"I'm sorry you still hurt over him, Ms. Edna." And Agatha could see that her mind was clear as a bell as she remembered her husband.

"Tom was my one true love," she said, her smile nostalgic. "He never cared a lick for all the gossips or busybodies, or the things people said. He always loved me. No matter what."

"That's sweet," Agatha said. "And very special. You're a lucky woman."

Edna looked at her and she could tell in an instant that whatever clarity she'd had was long gone.

"Yes, it was a lovely wedding, dear. The whole town

was there. And I'll never forget what Pastor Ebenezer Schrute said during the ceremony."

"What was that?" Agatha asked. She noticed Darleen had come out of the front of the house with a frantic look in her eyes, and then gave a visible sigh of relief when she saw Edna sitting on the porch with Agatha.

"Never be afraid to be the one who loves the other the most," Edna said.

"Makes sense," Agatha said. "I can see why people might be afraid to love if losing them hurts that bed."

"But worth it," Edna said, giving her a sweet, child-like smile. "You're a sweet girl, Elaine. You'd better go check on the baby. I think I hear her crying."

"Elaine?" Agatha said, her mouth going dry as dust.

"Ms. Edna," Darleen called out. "You know you're not supposed to leave the house without telling me. Now come on back. You missed your nap, and you'll be tired this afternoon when we go to the grocery store."

"I enjoyed our chat," Edna said, hefting her weight up off the stairs. "Bring that sweet baby over later if you get a chance."

Agatha watched as she went back to her house and introduced herself to Darleen as if it were the first time, and her eyes stung with the sadness of it all. Her thoughts were jumbled as she finished her coffee, but she kept going back to what Edna had said about Jim Brown killing his wife. Maybe that was worth looking into a little deeper. Just in case.

Liliana and I have loved sharing these stories in our Harley & Davidson Mystery Series with you.

There are many more adventures to be had for Aggie and Hank. Make sure you stay up to date with life in Rusty Gun, Texas by signing up for our emails.

Thanks again and please be sure to leave a review where you bought each story and, recommend the series to your friends.

Kindly,
Scott & Liliana

Enjoy this book? You can make a big difference

Reviews are so important in helping us get the word out about Harley and Davidson Mystery Series. If you've enjoyed this adventure Liliana & I would be so grateful if you would take a few minutes to leave a review (it can be as short as you like) on the book's buy page.

Thanks,
Scott & Liliana

Also by Liliana Hart

The MacKenzies of Montana

Dane's Return

Thomas's Vow

Riley's Sanctuary

Cooper's Promise

Grant's Christmas Wish

The MacKenzies Boxset

MacKenzie Security Series

Seduction and Sapphires

Shadows and Silk

Secrets and Satin

Sins and Scarlet Lace

Sizzle

Crave

Trouble Maker

Scorch

MacKenzie Security Omnibus 1

MacKenzie Security Omnibus 2

JJ Graves Mystery Series

Dirty Little Secrets

A Dirty Shame

Dirty Rotten Scoundrel

Down and Dirty

Dirty Deeds

Dirty Laundry

Dirty Money

A Dirty Job

Addison Holmes Mystery Series

Whiskey Rebellion

Whiskey Sour

Whiskey For Breakfast

Whiskey, You're The Devil

Whiskey on the Rocks

Whiskey Tango Foxtrot

Whiskey and Gunpowder

Books by Liliana Hart and Scott Silverii

The Harley and Davidson Mystery Series

The Farmer's Slaughter

A Tisket a Casket

I Saw Mommy Killing Santa Claus

Get Your Murder Running

Deceased and Desist

Malice In Wonderland

Tequila Mockingbird

Gone With the Sin

The Gravediggers

The Darkest Corner

Gone to Dust

Say No More

Lawmen of Surrender (MacKenzies-1001 Dark Nights)

Also by Louis Scott

Books by Liliana Hart and Scott Silverii

The Harley and Davidson Mystery Series

The Farmer's Slaughter

A Tisket a Casket

I Saw Mommy Killing Santa Claus

Get Your Murder Running

Deceased and Desist

Malice in Wonderland

Tequila Mockingbird

Gone With the Sin

Liliana Hart is a New York Times, USAToday, and Publisher's Weekly bestselling author of more than sixty titles. After starting her first novel her freshman year of college, she immediately became addicted to writing and knew she'd found what she was meant to do with her life. She has no idea why she majored in music.

Since publishing in June 2011, Liliana has sold more than six-million books. All three of her series have made multiple appearances on the New York Times list.

Liliana can almost always be found at her computer writing, hauling five kids to various activities, or spending time with her husband. She calls Texas home.

If you enjoyed reading *this*, I would appreciate it if you would help others enjoy this book, too.

Lend it. This e-book is lending-enabled, so please, share it with a friend.

Recommend it. Please help other readers find this book by recommending it to friends, readers' groups and discussion boards.

Review it. Please tell other readers why you liked this

book by reviewing. If you do write a review, please send me an email at lilianahartauthor@gmail.com, or visit me at http://www.lilianahart.com.

Connect with me online:
www.lilianahart.com
lilianahartauthor@gmail.com

facebook.com/LilianaHart

twitter.com/Liliana_Hart

instagram.com/LilianaHart

bookbub.com/authors/liliana-hart

Liliana's writing partner and husband, Scott blends over 25 years of heart-stopping policing Special Operations experience.

From deep in the heart of south Louisiana's Cajun Country, his action-packed writing style is seasoned by the Mardi Gras, hurricanes and crawfish étouffée.

Don't let the easy Creole smile fool you. The author served most of a highly decorated career in SOG buying dope, banging down doors, and busting bad guys.

Bringing characters to life based on those amazing experiences, Scott writes it like he lived it.

Lock and Load – Let's Roll.

Made in the USA
Middletown, DE
24 July 2021

44696223R00090